The Horse from Black Loch

D0315524

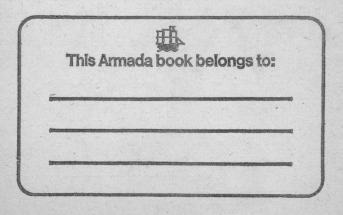

This Armada book belongs to:

Patricia Leitch is the author of the highly popular 'Jinny at Finmory' pony book series which she writes specially for Armada. *The Horse from Black Loch* was one of her earlier novels and received excellent reviews when first published in hardback under the title of 'The Black Loch'. Writing is now her full-time occupation, but she has also done all sorts of different jobs, including being a riding-school instructor, groom, teacher and librarian. She lives in Renfrewshire, Scotland, with a bearded collie called Meg.

Other pony books in Armada by Patricia Leitch
A Horse for the Holidays

'Jinny' at Finmory series
For Love of a Horse
A Devil to Ride
The Summer Riders
Night of the Red Horse
Gallop to the Hills

More of Patricia Leitch's books will be published in Armada

THE HORSE FROM BLACK LOCH

Patricia Leitch

Armada

The Horse from Black Loch was first published under the title
The Black Loch in hardback in 1963 by
William Collins Sons & Co. Ltd., London and Glasgow.
First published in Armada in the U.K. in 1979 by
Fontana Paperbacks,
14 St. James's Place, London SW1A 1PS

© Patricia Leitch 1963

Printed in Great Britain by
Love & Malcomson Ltd., Brighton Road,
Redhill, Surrey.

CHAPTER ONE

High above me a single swan flew like an unshriven ghost
through the lucid lime-yellow glow of the Highland evening. Swiftly the beat of its powerful wings carried it from
my sights as I hung out of the train window watching it.

The little train chugged over the bare Scottish moorland
and my eyes lost the black speck of the swan against the
brightness of the sunset glow. I pulled myself back into the
compartment where my cousins, Sara and Edgar, were
moaning about the slowness of the journey and the emptiness of their stomachs.

"The only thing I want is for this train to reach Gartleven," Sara was saying. "We're two hours late already."

Even as she spoke the train shuddered to a grinding halt.

"Not again!" Edgar exclaimed. "I'm starving. There's
nothing here to make them stop."

"You'd think they'd want to hurry up themselves," I
said, staring out over the bleak moorland. On the far skyline mountains were clumbered together in massed greys
and blacks and all around us stretched a wilderness of
bracken and purple heather which flowed like the tide
washing around the grey outcrops of rocks. The glow of
the evening was gradually fading into the first cold coming
of the night. "Say there's no one to meet us?" I asked.

"There must be," Sara said. "I remember when Daddy
and I were here before they met us at the station and it
took hours to reach Deersmalen. We couldn't possibly get
there by ourselves."

"We might have to," Edgar said. "Good job I've got
my compass."

"Compass!" snorted Sara. "You and your compass. You
couldn't even find your way down the garden with it."

"I could so. Peter Truman and I went for a hike one day with only my compass to guide us."

"Bet you just went round the rugby pitch," Sara narked.

" 'Course we didn't. We went through Branley and past the toll . . ."

Edgar was well launched on one of his endless, boring accounts of what he did at school. I studied my cousins. It had been Christmas when I had seen them last and now it was the middle of August, but they hadn't changed. Sara, at fifteen, was pink and fat with soft, brownish hair that hung loosely down her back. Edgar was twelve. He was very like Sara, clean and pink, and keen on his school.

I am fourteen. Unlike my cousins I am thin and small with straight black hair cut in a fringe across my forehead. I have grey eyes and the kind of face that makes people say, "What's the matter with you, Kay?" when all I'm doing is thinking.

Our fathers are brothers, and normally the Innes families spend their summer holidays together, usually at the seaside in Cornwall. But this year our parents had decided to tour the Continent uncluttered by their children and had packed us off to stay with our uncle in the north of Scotland. I was glad really. Even the thought of spending weeks in a car made me feel sick.

"And when we got back Mr. Kerr, our housemaster, said we'd put up a pretty good show," Edgar finished triumphantly.

"Don't believe you." Sara remained unconvinced. "Hey! We're off again."

The train shook violently then with a tremendous effort lurched forward and we resumed our slow progress across the moor.

"I never knew you'd been to Deersmalen before," I said to Sara.

"It's a while ago," she replied. "Daddy and I stayed three nights there. I only went with him because Mummy was in Chester, nursing Gran, and I couldn't be left alone.

It rained all the time and you couldn't see a thing for mist."

"Then you've met them all, Aunt Sadie and Uncle Vincent and the children?"

"Yes. Aunt Sadie was nice, round and twinkly, but Uncle Vincent was terrifying. Not a bit like our fathers. He's got a huge black beard."

"How old are the children?" Edgar asked.

"Shona will be thirteen now and Jamie is a year older, I think. Caroline is the eldest. She'll be fifteen or maybe sixteen by now. I liked her the best. The other two just ran wild. I don't think they even went to school."

"Good for them." I said. "But they must go to school now, mustn't they?"

"I don't think so. Uncle Vincent and the local minister teach them."

"I'm absolutely starving," Edgar groaned. "My stomach is aching and rolling like nothing on earth. Has no one anything left? Even an old, dried up cough sweet would be smashing."

Sara and I searched our pockets but found nothing to eat.

"Not a thing," I said. "We *must* be nearly there by now." The dark was closing in and only the heather glowed a luminous purple.

"Just think of the parents rotting in luxury in some French hotel," Sara said longingly.

"I'd rather be here," I said, and I meant it.

"I'd rather be anywhere where there's food," brooded Edgar.

"Steak and chips," I suggested, making my mouth water.

"I can remember one night at Deersmalen," Sara told us, "they had a huge dinner with wine and everything. I was too young to stay up for it but after we were meant to be in bed Jamie and Shona took me to a balcony where you could look down on the dining-hall and watch them eating. There was a great log fire with the flames roaring up into the blackness of the chimney, candles on the table and dead animals staring down at them from the walls and the wine burned like jewels in the cut crystal glasses."

"Dead animals," repeated Edgar in amazement.

Sara didn't seem to hear him. Her blue eyes were bright with excitement almost as if she could see what she was describing to us.

"There were heavy swords and round shields hanging from the walls and they gleamed bright in the shadows. Along one side of the room the curtains hung down to the floor, deep, heavy, maroon velvet. Uncle Vincent was at the head of the table, carving the meat. You could see the black hairs on the back of his hands and his black beard and his nose jutting out from his face like an eagle's beak. Then the clock struck and he put down his carving knife and said something we couldn't make out from the balcony. Everyone stood up and lifted up their glasses. 'To the One of the Black Loch,' Uncle Vincent said and they all raised their glasses and drank the toast. Then they sat down again and Daddy was smiling and shaking his head as if he'd been caught doing something silly."

"But the animals, the dead animals, why were they there?" Edgar demanded again.

"Oh, do be quiet, Edgar," I said but it was too late. Sara had heard him.

"What?" she said. "What's that?" And she looked at Edgar as if he had woken her from a dream.

"What dead animals? You know. You said they were hanging from the walls."

"Oh, stuffed heads, deer and foxes, and a wild cat as well, I think. They'd all got glass eyes which shone in the candlelight. Do you know I'd forgotten all that until I started talking and then it all came back. Strange."

"Yes," I said. "Very." But I believed her for I'd never heard Sara talk about anything really interesting in her life before. All she normally talked about was hockey and clothes and how she became tired quicker than most people. "It must be a colossal house to have a dining-hall. I'd no idea it was as big as that."

8

"It's stone with towers and pointed windows and masses of outbuildings all rotted and decaying. I can't remember much about the grounds, except for the pine trees. They seemed to be everywhere, stretching up into the mists."

"You'd think we'd have been to stay there before this," I said. "It sounds a super place for holidays."

"Uncle Vincent," said Edgar knowingly. "We heard Mum and Dad discussing whether they would let us come and stay this time. There was a frightful row when Dad left Deersmalen years ago and he's only been back once

since he left. That time when he went with Sara to sign some papers or something."

I wondered if my father too had fought with Uncle Vincent, because although I knew he had been born and brought up in the Highlands at the house called Deersmalen he hardly ever talked about his childhood there, and although we always sent birthday and Christmas presents to our cousins at Deersmalen I knew nothing at all about them. They were the Deersmalen children, as remote and mysterious as children from another land, another world almost.

"Perhaps Jamie or Shona will know more about it," I suggested hopefully.

As I spoke the train started to slow down. Edgar lowered the window and looked out.

"It's a station," he yelled. "Do you think it'll be ours?"

"Bound to be," I said.

"I should think it will be," Sara said with more authority but less vigour.

All our luggage was in the guard's van. The only thing we had with us was a shopping bag that had once held our lunch and a varied selection of magazines and comics, which, by now, were mostly coming to pieces and going tatty round the edges.

"I'll just take the comics with us," Edgar said, cramming them into the shopping bag. "You never know whether there'll be anything to read here or not."

The train stopped and by the asthmatic flickering of a gas lamp we were able to make out the word "Gartleven" printed in faded white letters on a blue board.

"This is it," Edgar shouted and swinging open the door he jumped down. Sara and I followed him out.

"Better see that all our luggage is here," Sara muttered as she ran towards the guard's van.

"Better had. My cricket bat is in one of the cases," Edgar agreed, running after her.

The train, never the speediest of transport, now had the settled look of a cat with her paws tucked in and Sara's mad rushing seemed to be quite unnecessary. I stood still and looked about me. There wasn't anything much to see—a cindered platform edged with wilted wallflowers, the name of the station lit by the solitary light and the little train just waiting. The darkness curved round, shading everything else from sight, but as far as I could see there was no one to meet us. I wriggled inside my clothes for the wind was cold and I turned my mind resolutely away from the thought of our dining-room at home, the sun shining in through the open french windows, flowers massed in white vases and the table set for dinner.

With a most untypical snort and flurry the train gathered itself together and went about its business, leaving Sara and Edgar surrounded by cases. I walked over to them.

"Well, there's no one here," I said.

"You don't say," Sara snapped.

"I should think . . ." but we never discovered what Edgar thought for out of the darkness a tall, angular man came striding towards us, a dog at his heels. He was wearing a heavy cloak that spread out behind him as he walked and in his hand he held a lantern.

"Do you think he's for us?" Sara asked anxiously. "What do you think he is, a gamekeeper?"

The man came straight towards us and as he drew nearer we could see that his face was tanned brown as leather and his eyes were the colour of peaty water flecked curiously with green lights.

He stopped in front of us and held up his lantern. For a second nobody spoke. I heard Edgar swallow, gulpingly, and Sara clear her throat ready to make a polite remark but it was the man who spoke first.

"I did not know that one of you had black hair," he said. "But who knows it may be a good thing in the end." His gaze moved from me to Edgar. "You are your father's son," he said, as if that was all that need ever be said about Edgar, and in a way it was. Then to Sara he said, "And you will be pleasant company for Miss Caroline."

We three stood like moths drawn by the light of his lantern, staring at him speechless.

"But I have not introduced myself. I am Fergus, ghillie at Deersmalen. I trust you all had a good journey?"

It had been a long, horrible journey but we all said yes we had had a good journey. Sara's agreement came out in her most English accent, Edgar's was muttered and mine was squeaky.

"Now I am surprised to hear that. There are many people who would be grumbling about a train that was two and a half hours late but I can see that you are not like that." Fergus's face creased into a network of wrinkles. He

11

laughed with his eyes and the long lines from his nostrils to his thin-lipped mouth deepened, just twisting the corners of his lips upwards.

For a second we stared at him, not quite sure whether to laugh or not.

"It was a rotten, lousy journey," Edgar said. "I've never been so hungry in my life before." Sara and I joined in his laughter.

"That is more like it," Fergus agreed as he picked up our cases. "There is still another hour to be endured but I dare say you will survive. You do not look as if you will die from starvation yet. I have the car waiting." And he led the way out of the station.

It was a large black car, with sweeping lines and a little silver horse on the bonnet. Once you got close to it you could see how old it really was. The paintwork was scratched and one of the back bumpers was crushed inwards.

"I will take the luggage in front with me and you shall sit in the back," Fergus said and opened one of the back doors for us. "Do not step on the running-board. Jamie has made a good job of sticking it on but it would not be up to your weight I'm thinking."

Giggling to ourselves, we climbed into the back of the car. Sara and Edgar went in first. I was just about to climb in after them when I realised that Fergus's dog was no longer with us.

"Where's your dog?" I asked him. "Can he come in the back with us?"

Fergus stopped piling our cases into the front of the car and, turning round, he looked me straight in the eyes.

"I had no dog with me," he said. "The lantern casts strange shadows. Maybe you are not yet used to its light."

"It wasn't the lantern," I exclaimed indignantly. "I saw it quite clearly when you came over at first. A big, grey Alsatian walking at your heels. You saw it too, didn't you?" I demanded into the dark cavern of the car. "The big Alsatian Fergus had with him when he came to meet us."

12

"No," Fergus said. "You're imagining things. I never saw a dog."

"Nor did I," Sara said. "There wasn't a dog or I'd have seen it."

"But I saw it," I repeated.

"Oh, get a move on and stop dithering," Edgar said irritably. "We'll never get any food tonight at this rate."

"You see," Fergus stated. "You were wrong. As I said there was no dog." And he finished piling the cases into the car.

"Then it must have been someone else's dog because I'm sure I saw one," I muttered, unconvinced. But I stopped arguing and climbed into the car, being careful not to step on the running-board.

The inside of the car was completely separate from the front. There was a sort of speaking tube for emergencies but that was all.

"If you turn the switch up," Fergus said, showing us the switch as he spoke, "you can speak to me and I can speak to you. But if you have something private to say or are bored with my noise you switch it down and you are alone."

He shut our door and going round to the driver's seat got in and started up the engine. The inside of the car was damp and cold. The leather of the seats was cracked and here and there loose springs made strained rings beneath it.

Sara shuddered and turning up the switch she asked how long it would be before we reached Deersmalen.

"About two hours is the time it takes the Master but I'm thinking tonight we will be hurrying." Fergus's disembodied voice sounded distant and echoing.

"Jolly good," Edgar said.

"You're starving," I said, getting it in before him.

Fergus meant what he'd said about hurrying. On the rough moorland road the car sprang and leapt and crashed down while we in the back were shaken to and fro like dice in a gambler's hand. Outside the moon had risen and was riding high above long veils of cloud. Through the car windows I saw the brackened moorland turn into wilder,

13

more mountainous country until our road wound its way between grey rocks silvered in the moonlight and streaked at intervals with the white flurry of falling water.

We were all asleep before we reached Deersmalen.

"We have arrived," Fergus said, opening the car door. I woke suddenly at the sound of his voice. I couldn't think where I was nor who Fergus was. For a second I cowered away from him. "You are not afraid?" he questioned. "You are at your uncle's house and you with the black hair have no cause for fear. Your father has been most generous to us for many years. Without him we might not have been able to go on."

"Daddy most generous?" I echoed, drugged with sleep. "What do you mean? And why is my black hair so special, lots of people have black hair."

My voice woke Sara.

"Are we there?" she asked, jumping up. "Gosh I'm glad. We'll all be black and blue after that. You need to buy a new car. Edgar, we're here." She shook Edgar by the shoulder, waking him.

Still half asleep, we fumbled our way out of the car. Edgar trod on the running-board and it came off.

"Jamie will not be pleased but do not worry. I do not think we will be needing the car again for some time. Jamie can stick it on again," Fergus said, and put the running board in the back of the car. Then he picked up our cases and led the way to the house.

Deersmalen seemed enormous. It stood black against the feathery darkness of the surrounding pines. Only the slate roof with its three pointed towers stood out against the moon-bright sky.

Fergus rang the heavy brass bell that hung from the wall and the noise broke into the silence, crashing and reverberating into the night. Almost at once the heavy oak door swung open.

"Come in, come in, come in. You're hours late, my dears. I've been worried stiff about you all. I can't tell you how glad I am to see you."

14

We trooped into the dimly lit hall and each in turn were smothered by the warm embrace of the little lady who had opened the door and whom I presumed to be Aunt Sadie. She wasn't much taller than myself but round and bright with twinkling blue eyes and yellow hair that stood up in twists and twirls all over her head.

"Now you must be Kay, and Edgar, and Sara. My, how you've grown, Sara! But there, Caroline is always telling me not to say that to people. And Kay, how like your Uncle Vincent you are. Your father always told us that in his letters but we didn't really believe him. Jamie will be so pleased to have another boy to talk to, Edgar. They're all in bed but you'll meet tomorrow. Now upstairs first and I've a meal waiting for you when you're ready. I'll show you your rooms and Fergus can bring your cases up later."

We followed her up the broad stairs that curved upwards with the lift and sweep of a gull's flight. Aunt Sadie seemed to bounce from step to step, talking all the time; asking after our mothers and fathers; telling us how she had always longed to see us and hoping that we would enjoy ourselves now that we were here.

We followed her down a long, high-ceilinged passage with doors on either side of it. She stopped at one and opened it.

"This is your room, Sara and Kay," she said. "I hope you don't mind sharing a bed but really the beds in this place are so enormous I just can't get bedclothes for them."

As she spoke she crossed the room, and, striking a match, she lit an oil lamp. The tiny crescent of fire flared upwards, lighting the room which was big and bare. The ceiling was decorated with ornate plasterwork. The walls were papered with thick, murky brown paper, peeling off at the corners, and hung with three oil paintings in elaborate gilt frames. One was of redcoats marching to battle, one of the wreck of a sailing ship on the rocks and the third of a stag being monarch of the glen-ish against a scarlet sunset.

15

"I know," said Aunt Sadie, seeing me looking at the paintings. "They're grim but I can't take them down, the faded patches of wallpaper look even grimmer. I shan't mind in the least if you shroud them with something."

The bed was vast and covered with a richly embroidered counterpane. There was a massive dressing-table with a tiny speckly mirror in it and a ponderous tallboy. The floor was polished wood with two shabby rugs on it which only succeeded in making it look more bare.

"Well, my dears, I'm afraid that's that." For a second Aunt Sadie looked wearily about her, but almost immediately she perked up again. "But the bed has an interior spring mattress. I just put my foot down about that. Now Edgar, I'll show you to your room. The bathroom is next door but one," Aunt Sadie called back to us.

Left alone Sara and I flopped down on our interior springs.

"Isn't it weird?" Sara exclaimed. "I can't remember it being anything like this when I was here before."

"I think it's terrific," I said. "What I can't understand is how I never knew that it was practically a castle. And what did Fergus mean about Daddy being generous?"

"Fergus is strange all right," Sara said. "The way he looks at you makes your blood run cold."

"I've never seen anyone who wore a cloak before."

"Nor me," Sara said. "Bags me first for the bathroom." And jumping up she scudded out through the door.

I took my jacket off and hung it over one of the bed-posts. Then I went over to the dressing-table and peered at my face in its dim, secret little glass. While I was standing there combing my hair there was a knock at the door. I turned, thinking it would be Fergus with the cases. "Come in," I shouted.

The door opened and a boy and girl of about my own age came in.

"Shh!" whispered the boy. "They think we're asleep. I'm Jamie Innes and this is Shona."

"Hullo," Shona said. "You must be Kay. I can just remember Sara and she had brown hair."

"That's right," I said. "Sara's in the bathroom."

"It doesn't matter," Jamie said. "It's you we wanted to see. Your father said in his letters that you were very like Dad and we wanted to see for ourselves."

"Your mother said the same thing," I told him. "But I don't see that it matters. Not enough for you to stay awake for."

"Oh, but it does matter," Shona said. "It's terribly important."

"It's just you being dark and having black hair like Dad when we're all blond like Mummy," Jamie said.

"That's right," Shona echoed her brother.

"Honestly I never met people who made such a fuss about nothing. Just because I'm supposed to look a bit like my uncle. It's mad."

"You don't understand," Shona began but Jamie interrupted her.

"Have you had your meal yet?" he asked, suddenly polite.

"Not yet. We've just arrived."

There was a slight sound from the passage.

"That'll be Sara. We'd better go," Jamie said. "See you properly tomorrow." And as silently as they had come, Jamie and Shona went.

"Was there someone in here?" Sara asked, coming back from the bathroom. "I thought I heard you talking."

"Shona and Jamie," I replied. "But they were meant to be asleep."

"They might have waited and let me meet them again," Sara complained. "What were they like?"

"Nice," I said. "They look as if they'll be good fun." I saw in my mind's eye the thin, tight figures of Jamie and Shona.

Jamie's dressing-gown, obviously a hand-down, had been girded tightly round his waist. Shona's had been too small so that her bony wrists stuck out from its shrunken sleeves

17

and its hem barely reached her knees. They were both blond. Shona had long, straight, silvery hair, an open expression and laughing blue eyes like her mother's. Jamie's hair was the dead shade of dank straw and it fell like a wing over his forehead. His eyes were blue but hard and glittering like sea-washed pebbles; his tanned skin was

tightly drawn over high cheekbones; his nose straight; his chin pointed; his whole face was ferret-sharp and cunning but there was a brightness about him that was instantly attractive. I had seen him for only a few minutes yet I was sure that he would be ready for anything at any minute of the day or night. Energy and life seemed to sparkle from him.

"Yes," I said again. "I bet you they'll be good fun."

"I liked Caroline best when I was here," Sara said in her primmest tones.

"You would," I sneered and dashed out to the bathroom.

When we got downstairs Edgar was already stuffing himself with food.

"Couldn't wait," he mumbled. "I was starving."

"Sit down, dears, and begin." Aunt Sadie came bustling in carrying two plates of bacon, eggs, baked beans and fried tomatoes.

While we ate, Aunt Sadie sat down at the table with us and talked and talked and talked. About Deersmalen, about how far away the nearest shop was, about how difficult schooling was for Jamie and Shona, but most of all about how glad she was that we had at last come to stay with them.

I had just reached the comfortably full stage and was sitting back and wondering if I should have another piece of bread and jam when Uncle Vincent came in.

He paused for a second, looking down at us, and then, urging us not to get up, he shook hands with Sara and Edgar and told them how welcome they were at Deersmalen. But when he reached my side of the table and stretched out his hand to me I stood up and shook hands with him. Somehow I felt it would have been all wrong to have remained seated while I spoke to him for the first time.

"For many years I have been deeply indebted to your father," he said, and his voice rang in the room like the brass bell outside. "There is nothing within my power which I would not do for you. While you are here Deersmalen is your home. You could not be more welcome, Kay."

I could think of nothing to say in reply. My mouth had gone dry and I could feel the thumping of my heart in my side, for what they had all been saying was true. I *was* very like my Uncle Vincent. He stood well over six feet tall. He was broad-shouldered and black bearded. Yet when I looked into his eyes it was almost like looking into a mirror. They were the same deep grey as my own; his eyebrows arched above them in lines identical to my own; my nose jutted out as his did; my lips were curved and moulded as his and our hair was black as jet.

"You are the spitting image of him," Sara said as we got ready for bed. "I would never have believed it if I hadn't seen you both."

"Well, he is Daddy's brother," I said. "There's no need to go on about it."

"I'm not," said Sara in righteous indignation. "I'm just saying it's strange, that's all."

"There's nothing strange about it," I began as Sara flung herself on to our interior spring mattress and burrowed down under the bedclothes.

"I'm first in. You'll need to put out the lamp," she triumphed.

"O.K., I don't mind."

I fastened up my pyjama jacket and, walking over to the tallboy, I turned out the oil lamp. The room was instantly filled with the white gleam of the moon.

"Draw the curtains," Sara said. "I could never sleep with the moon shining in on me like that."

"I like it," I said. "But I'll draw them if you want me to."

I drew one curtain over the high window and stood looking out of the silvered world beneath me. There was a stretch of rough grass and then the pine trees grew thick and close together. Their sweeping branches crossed and interlaced into blackness which even the moonlight could not penetrate.

As I stood gazing down a shape moved out from between the pine trunks a low-slung, liquid moving greyness. It came out on to the grass and I saw that it was a dog, a grey Alsatian. It was the dog that I had seen earlier in the evening with Fergus. I knew I had been right. The dog stood for a second, one forepaw lifted up, its mouth open, panting, and its curved white teeth glinting in the moonlight.

20

"Sara," I whispered urgently. "Come quickly. It's that dog. The one I saw at the station. Come and see. It must have followed us here."

"What d'you say?" Sara muttered irritably.

But she was too late. Another grey shape moved in the darkness of the trees. The dog turned and slunk back into the woods to join it. There had been two Alsatians. But now there was nothing but silence, white moonshine and the black pines. I shuddered and as quickly as I could I drew the curtain across the window, ran over the wooden floor and into bed.

"What did you say?" Sara asked.

"It was that dog out there under the pines. The one I saw at the station. Only this time there were two of them. If you'd come when I told you to you would have seen them."

"Rubbish! It's your imagination."

"I tell you I saw them just now." But I was too tired to argue. "Whether you believe me or not, they're out there in the wood and I saw them."

"Rubbish," Sara said again and, turning her back to me, she slept.

CHAPTER TWO

"Meet you at the front door as soon after breakfast as you can make it," Jamie said. He had stopped me on the stairs on my way down to breakfast. "Just yourself, mind. Not the other two."

"O.K.," I agreed and he hurried on upstairs.

"Breakfast's in the kitchen," Aunt Sadie called. "Down the passage to the right, Kay, and watch the steps."

I hurried along the passage, almost tripped over the two steps and half fell into the kitchen. Everyone except Jamie was sitting round the table eating.

"Good morning, Kay, you're late," Uncle Vincent said.

"Oh, Vin!" Aunt Sadie exclaimed. "Give the child a chance. Come and sit down, Kay. This is Caroline and I believe that you've already met Shona and Jamie."

I shook hands with Caroline who said she was pleased to meet me. She had silvery hair like Shona's but she looked neater and more Sara's type of person.

"I had to send Jamie back upstairs," Aunt Sadie told me as she filled my plate with porridge. "Coming down to breakfast in that disgusting old dressing-gown."

I thanked her for the porridge and, pulling in my chair, I started to eat it just as Jamie came back in.

"That do?" he asked his mother.

"It's better," she said, looking doubtfully at the tattered kilt he was wearing.

"Front door after breakfast," Shona whispered to me as she leant over to get the marmalade.

"Don't whisper, Shona," Aunt Sadie said automatically. "And what are you planning to do today?" she asked us.

"Jamie and I have a lot to do," Shona said. "We've things to see to."

"No one ever thought that Jamie and you would be

available for any civilised occupation," Caroline said. "It's ridiculous the way you two do exactly what you like."

"Don't be a dog in the manger, Caro," Jamie said. "You do what you like. We do what we like."

Caroline ignored him. Turning to Sara she said, "I'll show you around afterwards, if you like. It was such miserable weather last time you were here that you never saw a thing."

Jamie winked at me and Shona grinned, welcoming me into the charmed circle of their company. Outside the sky was blue, the sun shone and the noise of birds racketed against the window.

"If you help me with the dishes and leave your rooms tidy that'll do for today. Midge is coming," Aunt Sadie said as she cleared the table.

"Who's Midge?" I asked Jamie.

"Midge?" he said. "She comes and helps Mum when we can afford her but that's not often."

"Oh," I said, remembering what Sara had told us on the train and wondering how my cousins could live in a house like Deersmalen and yet be as poor as they seemed to be.

Caroline washed, Sara and I dried and Shona put the dishes away.

I made our bed quickly and managed to slip away while Sara was still talking to Aunt Sadie. I dashed downstairs, through the hall and out into the brightness of the morning. Shona was waiting for me.

"Buck up," she said. "Before anyone sees us. This way." She ran quick and lithe before me and I followed as quickly as I could. She sped over the unkempt lawn, round the corner of an outbuilding and stopped in a cobbled yard.

"Jamie," she yelled. "Jamie."

From the darkness of one of the doorways came Jamie, his eyes bright and his lips curling in laughter. "I've fed the hens, collected the eggs and seen to the goat."

"Wonders never cease," said Shona.

"As if I didn't do it every day," Jamie said.

23

"Huh!" snorted Shona. "I like that."

"Now don't start," Jamie said. "What shall we do! Kay, what shall we do? We can fish or swim or sail or ride. All the extravagant pleasures of the rich are here for you to choose from. I can show you a golden eagle's nest or a wild cat's kittens. I can take you through caves known only to Shona and myself. I can show you standing stones so old that for centuries no man has known how they came to be on the moor. Or we could spend all day sleeping in the sun. The choice is yours."

"First," I said, "I'd like to know the answers to some things I don't understand."

"Trust a woman to want the one thing she can't have. Well, I'll do my best. Ask away," Jamie said.

"Why have we never been here before?"

"Because you never came," Jamie said. "Next question, please."

"But why did we never come?"

"You should know. We always thought you were too stuck up to bother with us," Shona replied.

"But I never really knew about you. Sara and Edgar think there was a row between your father and our fathers years ago."

"We know but we can't tell you," Jamie said. "You know your father sends us money. That's how Caro goes to boarding school and a fat lot of good it does her. Well, we wouldn't dream of taking it if it were only for that but there's something else. A sort of family responsibility which your father and Sara's and Edgar's father should have shared with Dad. Only they didn't. They thought he should throw the whole thing up and they left Deersmalen and Dad to get on with it as best they could. But now your father sends us money."

"Tell me what it was the family thing that they should have stayed for," I demanded.

"We can't. Only Dad or Fergus can tell you. But for goodness' sake don't ask them or they'll know we've been talking about it and Shona and I would be nearly murdered."

"Promise," Shona insisted. "Promise you won't ask them."

"O.K., I promise."

"What else do you want to know?" asked Jamie.

"Why is there such a fuss about my black hair and the way I look like Uncle Vincent?"

"It's the Innes family face," Shona said. "It just seems to have skipped Jamie and Caro and me. We thought it had missed a whole generation until we saw you last night."

"We used to have lots of portraits of ancestors that hung in the dining-hall but they're all sold now. Well, they were nearly all like you and Dad, black hair, grey eyes and beak noses," said Jamie.

"I like your cheek," I exploded. "Just because I've got a bone in my nose doesn't mean to say that I've got a great whopping nose like your father's."

"Keep your hair on. Anything else? If so make it snappy or we'll have Caro and Co. here before we're away."

"Yes," I said. "Fergus's dogs. I saw one at the station last night. I knew I'd seen it but Fergus lied about it. He said there was no dog with him. Then last night looking through the bedroom window I saw two dogs at the edge of the pines."

Out of the corner of my eye I saw Shona and Jamie glance quickly at one another and Jamie shake his head very slightly. So I knew that whatever the truth was about the great, grey dogs I wasn't to hear it.

"They're Alsatians," Jamie said. "Fergus would send it home by itself because he wouldn't want you lot swarming over it. They're not that kind of dog. They belong to Fergus. Even Dad doesn't have anything to do with them."

"All Fergus had to do was explain to us. I'm not the sort of person that flings my arms round every dog I meet," I said indignantly. "It was silly trying to pretend that he hadn't a dog with him when I'd seen it."

"Oh, come on," Shona exclaimed. "Let's do something.

I'm bored standing here. Let's go to the sea. We haven't been for ages."

"It's up to Kay," Jamie said. "I don't mind what we do."

"Oh yes, the sea," I said. "I never knew it was as close as that."

"We'll take a picnic," Jamie said. "You take the eggs in, Shona, and scrounge some food while Kay and I fetch the ponies."

"Ponies?" I echoed.

"We've got six Highland ponies. We all use them instead of bikes or the car. They're cheaper and they're the best thing for getting about on up here." Jamie took three rope halters from a hook on the wall and a scoopful of oats from a bin. "Can you ride?" he asked.

"Yes," I said. "I ride a lot at a riding school at home."

"Just as long as you can stick on."

I followed Jamie along a narrow track through the pine trees. The ground was a thick, squelchy carpet of pine needles and the dead lower branches of the pine trees caught in my hair, the brittle twigs snapping off as I pushed my way through. We came out of the pine trees on to a hill-side of short, well-cropped grass.

"I'll call them," Jamie said. "They don't always come for me. It was Fergus who taught them to come. But I'll try." And putting his cupped hands to his mouth he called the ponies. "C'up on, c'up on the ponies. C'up the little horses," he yelled.

I stood watching the hillside for any sign of the ponies. Then suddenly I saw them dashing over the skyline. They came galloping down towards us, tossing their heads, shaking their long manes and bucking for joy as they came.

"They're coming," Jamie said, grinning, pleased with himself. "You can ride Polly, the white one. Mum usually rides her so you're bound to be able to manage her."

The six ponies galloped right up to us and then propped to a sudden standstill with stiff, outstretched forelegs. There was one white pony, one grey speckled with beige dapples, three yellow duns with black manes and tails and one dark brown one.

Jamie took the scoop of oats and caught the white pony. "Polly," he said, handing the halter rope to me. "Shona can ride Turk." He put a halter on a thick-set yellow dun. "And I'll take Maggie." He caught the dark brown pony for himself.

"We ride?" he asked. I nodded. "Then back we go." He sprang lightly on to Turk, holding Maggie's halter rope in one hand. Not to be outdone, I leaped up on to Polly.

When we got back to the yard Shona was waiting for us. She was holding a small black dog in her arms.

"I got caught," she said.

"You see," Jamie said as he slid to the ground, "if I don't do everything myself."

"It's a pity," said Shona darkly, "that we're not all as clever as you. Mum saw me. We've to go to the shop and get three pounds of flour but it'll do on our way back and we're to take Merchant."

Merchant I presumed was the black dog.

"You'll need to take him because I'm riding Maggie and she hates it when he holds on with his claws."

"Oh, I don't mind. I've put a lead on him to-day," Shona said. "I got some food—cheese and rolls and apples."

Jamie put the scoop down and, handing the halter ropes to me, he went in for a dandy brush. He came back and gave the ponies a quick brush over.

"That'll do," he said as Shona neatly and quickly took their halters off and put their bridles on.

"Aren't you going to change?" I asked. Jamie and Shona were both wearing kilts.

"Change?" queried Shona, aghast. "You mean into jodhpurs? 'Course not. We don't possess such things. We don't have saddles either. We just ride the way we are, bareback."

"Oh!" I said, aware that I had put my foot in it.

Jamie took the haversack of food, swung it over his back

and jumped on to Maggie. Shona sat Merchant on Turk's withers and jumped up after him. "Now just cling on to-day," she told him severely. "We don't want another day like the last time we took you, trying to get off every time you thought you smelt a rabbit." The little black dog yawned derisively, showing a tiny pink tongue and minute pin-pricks of teeth. I scrambled up on Polly and we set off.

Jamie first, Shona next, holding her reins in one hand and Merchant's lead wrapped round the other, and myself last. We went along a dark, narrow path through the pines and then out on to the hillside.

"We canter here," Jamie shouted back to me and almost at once we were cantering. The ponies bucketed along, their heads down between their knees, leaving only a hairy lump of wither in front of us. The hillside was criss-crossed with dry stone walls which we jumped as we came to them. After the first three walls I decided that Polly could look after herself and I relaxed and enjoyed my ride. We cantered on for ages, far longer than I had ever cantered before, but at last the ground became too rough and Jamie pulled Maggie to a walk.

"They can fairly move for all the size they are," he said, patting her neck. "But some day I shall have a good horse, worth riding."

The ponies walked out surefootedly over the rough ground and we rode in silence.

We seemed to ride for hours and I was just wondering how much longer I could stand the ache in my legs without getting off to stretch them when Jamie announced that we were nearly there.

"We go up to the top there and then we need to get off and lead the ponies down the track to the shore."

We reached the crest of land and there before us was the sea. A wide strip of shingle stretched out to water of a translucent silver, edged with bright saffron seaweed. Smooth and polished as a mirror, the water reached as far as the eye could see, to the very skyline edging of dusk blue mountains. So high were we that we looked down on the backs of the gulls, swooping, soaring and drifting above the shingle.

The drop to the shore seemed almost perpendicular.

"Where's the path down?" I asked apprehensively.

"Well, there's not much of one but you can get down. We've done it lots of times but you have to watch the ponies," Jamie said.

Jamie was right about the track. We all stumbled and slipped our way down it. For most of the time I was spread-eagled against the rockface, leaving Polly to find her own way down as best she could. But at last we reached the shore.

"Always when I get down and I look back up I wonder how I do it," Jamie said.

"No you don't," Shona contradicted. "You just think, that was pretty good, Jamie Innes, not many other people could have done that. You can't fool me. I know you too well."

Jamie just grinned at her. "Come on and water the ponies," he said.

We led them to a pool of fresh water. "Just take Polly's bridle off," Shona directed me. "We always turn them loose here. There's nowhere they can go to."

The three ponies, set free, drank deeply then started to nibble the spiny thistles that grew on the shingle.

"We leave them here," Shona said, "and go round over the rocks for our lunch. There's a bit of sand there but if we took that lot with us they'd muck it up in no time." And she led the way over the rocks to a crescent cove of white sand.

"Just enough for us," Jamie said as we all flopped down.

"Why is it white?" I asked, running a handful of the fine, sun-warmed sand between my fingers.

"Don't know," Jamie replied. "All the beaches round here are."

Shona opened the haversack and handed us each two flat morning rolls, a lump of cheese and an apple. "There's a bottle of fizz for after," she said. "But we'll eat first and then it won't get filled with disgusting bits from everyone's lunch."

"Having a hygienic day today, Shona dear?" Jamie asked. "You'd think Kay and I had foot and mouth."

After we had finished the food and the fizz, Shona and I lay back on the sand. The sea glinted and sparkled before us, lying still as a vast mill pond. Herring gulls squabbled amongst the sea wrack and an occasional gannet soared overhead.

Jamie sat still for about five minutes and then he jumped to his feet.

"Let's do acrobats," he suggested.

"You do," Shona told him. "Kay has never seen you before. She's bound to be impressed. People always are the first time. Me, I'm just bored."

He started with several ordinary cartwheels and handstands. "That's just to warm up," he said.

It was. He got quicker and quicker until I could hardly follow his movements. His tight, wiry body doubled and twisted and turned. He could spin over in the air without touching the ground with his hands. Over and over he went. He somersaulted rapidly along the sand, stood stiff as a tin soldier on his head, then walked towards us on his hands. He sprang upright and grinning from ear to ear shook the sand out of his hair.

"Good?" he asked Shona.

"Not bad," she said. "I've seen you better."

"Sand's not the best thing."

"It's all so that he can join a circus," Shona told me. "He's terrified that we ever have to leave Deersmalen and they try to make him work indoors. He thinks a circus is the only kind of life he could stand."

Jamie flopped down beside us. "Stow it," he said. "It sounds fantastic put in cold blood like that. Merchant's been in the water."

The little black dog came scampering out of the sea, wagging his curly tail.

"He does enjoy it," Shona said. "We should bring him more often. He was really quite good on Turk today."

"Look," said Jamie, jumping to his feet and pointing out to sea. "A boat."

Shona and I looked to where he was pointing. I could only see a black dot far out on the water.

"Coming in too," Jamie reported, shading his eyes against the sun. "Can't think who it can be. It's not the Craig Garth boat, is it?"

"No, too small," Shona said.

"It's Fergus!" Jamie yelled. "It is. I can see his cloak and there's a Grey One sitting in the bows." Jamie ran down to the sea's edge, shouting and waving his arms to attract Fergus's attention.

"It is him. He's coming in. Oh joy!" and Shona too ran down to the sea with Jamie.

Swiftly the little rowing boat drew in to the shore. It was Fergus. Even I could see him now and with him was one of his grey Alsatians. Jamie ran into the water and helped Fergus to ground the boat. The grey dog lay down in the bottom of the boat, its great head stretched out on its powerful legs.

"We never thought we'd see you here today," Jamie said.

"No," Fergus agreed. "But the sun was warm and my bones felt the need of a little sea air." He sat down on the

31

sand beside me and settled his cloak about himself. "I am glad to see that your cousins are looking after you," he said. "Do you like Deersmalen?"

"Oh yes," I said. "It's a wonderful place. I'd love to live here for ever."

"You have not seen it in the winter when the very birds freeze to death on the branches of the trees and icicles hang from the manes of the ponies so that you hear the thin chime of their movements coming to you over the white land. Guard your heart. Love of Deersmalen is not to be taken upon oneself lightly."

"But it's the only thing worth having," Jamie murmured, staring out over the sun-netted sea.

"You exaggerate," Fergus said. "Your cousin Edgar has spent the whole day practising bowling. To him cricket is of great importance."

"Ugh!" Jamie exclaimed in disgust.

"Do not be intolerant. It is a weakness."

"I'm not, but cricket, ugh!"

"Now that I am here," Fergus asked, "what shall I do? I am yours to command."

"Call in the seals," pleaded Shona. "Please, please, Fergus."

"Oh yes, Fergus," Jamie agreed. "Please, Fergus, Kay would love to see that. She'll never have seen anything like that in her life before."

"I've seen seals at the zoo," I said, doing my best to keep my end up, but they only laughed.

"I shall call in the seals then."

Fergus stood up and walked down to his boat. He spoke to his dog and it followed him back up the sand. When Merchant saw the great, grey dog he ran whimpering to Shona, asking her to pick him up.

"Beneath the rock," Fergus commanded and the dog walked across and lay down under the rocks. "They would not have passed him," Fergus said to Jamie. "Now we are ready."

Fergus took a silver pipe from his belt and placing it to

his mouth he ran his lips along it. An ascending scale of music escaped into the summer afternoon.

Crouching down, Fergus began to play. High and liquid the music rose in the still summer air. It sang of the running of fish in the unknown depths of the sea; of dark under-water caves known to no man; of great beaches where the surge crashed in upon the strand and of the first blind whimperings of new life. All these things I heard in it but there was much I could not understand. Music that rose and fell, crying with the restless knowledge of things long

forgotten by Man. Things we knew once, long ago, when we slopped and fell at the sea's edge, in our struggle to reach the land.

"They're coming," Shona breathed and, far out, breaking the looking-glass calm of the sea, were the sleek domed heads of the seals.

Fergus played on until the music seemed to forge invisible chains that drew the seals inwards towards us. They were all about the water's edge now, their eyes huge, dark pools, their long whiskers quivering, their whole bodies streamlined with the wash of the sea. The music cried to the hunger in

33

their beseeching eyes. Relentlessly the pipe drew them to Fergus.

At last, one bolder than the rest, surged up the sands, grunting, and came to rest only a few feet from Fergus. The others followed until all the sand was filled with seals.

The music changed. It became gentle and soft and easy. The sea world of which it sang was now languorous and peaceful. The seals stayed like graven statues without wills of their own.

Fergus took the pipe from his lips and looked about him.

"And now," he said in a low whisper, "our knives would have been at their throats. The sand would have lain scarlet under the moon tonight and the threat of famine would have been lifted from the people." The grey dog waiting under the rock heard Fergus's voice and sat erect, hackles raised, lips drawn back. "They would have said the Sea Gods had been kind to them. But that is long ago. Now I only play my pipe at the bidding of a child."

Suddenly Fergus sprang upright and throwing out his arms he released the seals from his spell.

"Get back to the sea, you foolish people," he cried. "Get back and stay."

The seals turned in a body and slithering, humping and shuffling they burst back into the sea. Once they had reached deep water they turned and watched us again with their dark, calm eyes.

"How many?" Fergus asked, slipping his pipe back into his belt.

"Twenty-four," Jamie told him.

"Not bad, not bad at all," Fergus said. "And how did you like the calling in of the seals?" he asked, turning to me.

But I had no answer. I hardly believed what I had seen. But I knew that I was half afraid of Fergus. I had no way of knowing what power he had used to call in the seals.

"It was terrific," I muttered inadequately.

"You are right. There has always been terror in it," Fergus agreed. "Now I must go and you too if you are to get the flour for your mother."

"Gosh! I'd forgotten all about it," Shona exclaimed, jumping to her feet. "Thank you, Fergus. I do wish you would get me a baby seal so that I could tame it. I keep asking you but you never do and I would love one."

"Thank you, Fergus," Jamie said. "They came quickly today, didn't they?"

"They were curious to see Kay," Fergus said and he smiled at me, his eyes a sparkling green. Then, calling his dog, he walked back to his boat, pushed it out by himself, jumped in and rowed away.

"Of course," Jamie said, "you'll not mention any of this at home."

"Of course not," I said.

"Not a word to Sara or Edgar. No hinting and making them suspicious."

"No," I said again. "Of course not."

"Anyway that's the last we'll see of Fergus for a bit. He's going away," Jamie said.

"No he's not," Shona contradicted him. "He's going somewhere first with Dad and we've to go with them. Dad promised."

"But not Kay," said Jamie. "She'll not be coming."

"Why not?" Shona demanded. "Fergus has never called in the seals before for anyone but us. I bet Dad would take her."

"Well, we could ask him," Jamie admitted grudgingly. "But I doubt it."

"Where are you going to anyway?" I asked. "Cheek of you both talking about me as if I wasn't here."

"Never you mind," Jamie told me, grinning. "Come on and catch the ponies or the shop will be shut before we get there and then there'll be a row with Mum."

I hurried after them, determined that where Jamie, Shona, Fergus and Uncle Vincent were going, I was going too.

CHAPTER THREE

The next day Jamie asked his father if I could go with them.

"We'll be away two nights," Jamie told me afterwards. "We're taking tents with us and pack ponies. Dad says you can come. Even if I hadn't asked him he was going to take you."

"When are we going?" I asked.

"When the time is right," Jamie said and would say no more.

Four days later Aunt Sadie found out about our proposed journey. She found Edgar sitting alone on the front door steps. He told her that he was fed up, bored and miserable; that he hated Deersmalen; that Caroline and Sara didn't want him and that Uncle Vincent, Jamie, Shona, Fergus and myself were going on a camping expedition and wouldn't take him with us.

Aunt Sadie was shocked to the depths of her hospitable soul. She took Edgar in, gave him a glass of lemonade and some chocolate biscuits and then she found Caroline and Sara and organised them into playing cricket with Edgar. Sara told me about this afterwards but Aunt Sadie spoke to us first. She was waiting for us when we got back at night.

"And where have you three been today?" she asked, folding her arms and perching on the end of the kitchen table.

"Sheep," said Jamie. "We've been helping Sandy Duncan bring in his hoggs for market."

"Oh, so you have, have you?" demanded his mother, her eyes flashing. "And I suppose you never thought that while you were running wild out there, you, as the only son of Deersmalen, had a duty towards your guests?"

"But we had Kay with us," Jamie began indignantly.

"It's not Kay I'm talking about. It's Edgar. I should be very surprised if you two had even spoken to each other since Edgar came."

"But, Mum, all he wants to do is throw that cricket ball about. Honestly, he'd have hated being with us today."

"Did you ask him?"

"No," admitted Jamie. "But, you see, I just knew he wouldn't want to come."

"You knew nothing of the sort. You're becoming so selfish that you think of nobody except yourself. I'm ashamed of you, Jamie, and I'll have no more of it. From now on you'll make friends with Edgar and you'll take him with you wherever you're going during the day. Do you understand?"

"I suppose so," said Jamie ungraciously.

"And that's not all," continued Aunt Sadie. "What is this story Edgar told me about a trek you're going on with your father and Fergus? It's strange the way I'm always the last one to hear about these things."

"Oh, it's nothing, really," Shona said. "Just that they promised to take us camping. It was all arranged ages ago."

Aunt Sadie was now bustling around, setting the table for supper. She spread out the red-and-white tablecloth with a flourish and banged down the mats.

"If it was arranged as long ago as that," she said, "you won't be able to change your plans now, will you?"

"Oh no," Jamie agreed with her. "Everything is settled."

"Then Kay won't be able to go with you, will she?" demanded Aunt Sadie, clashing the salt and pepper down on the table.

Jamie, Shona and I looked at each other. We were trapped.

"That's different," Jamie began. "You see, we sort of thought before that Kay might want to come with us."

"In other words Kay is going with you?"

"That's right," said Shona, relieved. "Jamie, Kay and I."

Aunt Sadie shook her head sadly at us. "You're not going to try and tell me that Edgar doesn't want to go camping

37

with you?" No one answered her. "Then I'll tell you some-thing. Unless Edgar goes camping with you, no one is going. I'll speak to your father about it tonight."

"But, Mum, Edgar can't possibly come with us. It's not that we don't want him. He can come anywhere else with us. Everywhere else with us. But truly he can't come camp-ing with us," Jamie protested.

Aunt Sadie ignored him. "Supper will be ready in half an hour," she said. "I want you all washed and changed by then. You stink of sheep."

"Please, Mum, do try to understand. It's something special. Edgar just can't come with us," Shona pleaded.

"Go and get changed at once." Aunt Sadie turned on us, thoroughly roused. "And not another word from any of you. I can't tell you how furious I was today when I found Edgar sitting there alone as miserable as anything and five other children in the house, three of them my own. I'm utterly ashamed of you all."

Silently we left the kitchen and went upstairs.

"Will Edgar want to come?" Jamie asked, clutching at straws.

"Bound to," I said gloomily. "It's just the sort of thing he'd love to tell them about at school."

"Then we've had it," Shona said.

"Would it be any use if I didn't come?" I asked them.

"Not now," Jamie replied. "Once Mum gets an idea into her head nothing will shift it. We either don't camp at all or Edgar comes with us."

"Jamie," exclaimed Shona suddenly. "What will Fergus say?"

"Don't," said Jamie. "I can't bear to think of it. I knew this was the kind of thing that would happen. I knew it whenever we got the letter asking if you could all come here." And sunk in gloom Jamie wandered away down the passage.

Uncle Vincent was in a good mood at supper. He told us stories of his boyhood at Deersmalen. How my father,

Sara's and Edgar's father and he himself, had all spent their childhood here.

"Goodness knows how any of us grew up," he said laughing. "The times we were nearly killed! We were away for days sometimes and our mother never knew when she would see us next. Your father," he said to Sara and Edgar, "was the worst of all. If he picked up a gun it went off, if he sat on a horse it bolted with him and he'd only to cross a bridge for it to collapse under him. Accident prone you'd call it today."

It wasn't until the end of the meal that Aunt Sadie mentioned our camping.

"I was hearing today that you're going camping," she said lightly.

"That's right, dear," said Uncle Vincent. "We're going up north. Depends on Fergus when we set off. Just a quick trip, two or three days."

"And Kay's going with you?" Aunt Sadie asked casually.

"That's right," said Uncle Vincent. "While she is here I'd like her to see everything. She has had to wait a long time to see the lands of her family. Fourteen years is a long exile. Yes, Kay will certainly be coming with us."

"Then Edgar will be going with you too?" Aunt Sadie said in the kind of voice that wasn't asking at all but was telling just exactly what was going to happen. "You'd like to go, wouldn't you, Edgar?"

" 'Course," Edgar muttered. "It would be smashing."

Uncle Vincent gazed down at Edgar a frown darkening his face. "I had not planned to take the boy," he murmured, more to himself than to us. "There is little Innes blood in his veins and much harm could come from idle watching."

"Oh, Vin, don't be so ridiculous. What harm could a twelve-year-old child do?" demanded Aunt Sadie. "He's your guest every bit as much as Kay. Of course he must go with you. There is no question of leaving him behind. I won't hear of it."

Uncle Vincent said nothing and Edgar took his silence for consent.

39

"Then I can really go?" he demanded. "Oh, I'll absolutely love it. I've always wanted to go on a proper camping expedition. Thanks terrifically, Aunt Sadie."

"Caroline and Sara, would you like to go too?" asked Aunt Sadie who was obviously set on turning the whole thing into a vast family outing.

"No thank you," Sara said.

"Not likely," echoed Caroline. "Ugh, just imagine wanting to go and sleep in tents when you don't need to."

After supper, Jamie, Shona and I went to look for Fergus. We found him in one of the outhouses, trimming Polly's feet. He looked up at our approach.

"You do not need to tell me," he said, his face grim. "Your father has already been here. When will you ever understand that it is loose talk that brings about these things? There should have been no talk about it. All was arranged. Your father would have told your mother the night before we left and all would have been well. But no, you must talk about it. Sometimes I think you will never learn to hold your tongues." Jamie fiddled with his watch strap, not looking at Fergus, and Shona and I stroked Polly's hard, hairy neck "No one can blame the boy for wanting to come too. It has always been the way of boys to come too. It is you with whom I am displeased. Edgar should have heard no word of our going."

"We're sorry," Jamie muttered. "We didn't mean to . . ."

But Fergus ignored him. "If it had been possible," he continued, "we would not have gone. We would have gone camping and that would have been all. But your father feels that it is time that we went as arranged. So I charge you all," and Fergus's eyes drew the unwilling attention of Shona, Jamie and myself, and held our gaze as he spoke – "let us have no more of this unnecessary talking." We nodded dumbly. "Now leave me for I have much to do before the morning."

Fergus turned away from us and, lifting Polly's off forehoof, began to trim it with his short, curved knife.

We spent the rest of the evening helping Aunt Sadie to

40

clean silver and listening to Edgar's excited talk about our camping expedition. Jamie and Shona hardly opened their mouths. They had obviously taken Fergus's warning to heart. I too had obviously taken Fergus's warning to heart. I too was silent, knowing that I had told Sara about our proposed camping expedition and that she must have told Edgar.

We all went to bed early, Sara telling everyone that the fresh air was making her so terribly tired.

When we got to bed she fell asleep immediately and left me to toss and turn as I thought about all the mysteries of Deersmalen. The more I wondered about them the more muddled I became. I couldn't think why Daddy had never told me about his boyhood here, or why he sent money to Uncle Vincent. I remembered Fergus's words to Shona and Jamie, "Your father feels that it is time we went as arranged," and I remembered the seals, how Fergus had called them to him out of the empty ocean. I tried to put it all out of my mind but I couldn't. I tried counting sheep and making my mind a blank but it was no good. I was as wide awake as ever. Then I thought I would like a drink of water and once I had thought about it I knew I would never sleep without one.

I slipped out of bed and as quietly as I could I tiptoed across the room and out into the corridor. I thought of having a drink in the bathroom, but remembering Shona's story about the toads they found in the water tank that supplied the bathroom, I decided to go downstairs for a drink. I reached the kitchen and filled a glass with water, drank it and started back upstairs.

I was still not very sure which rooms were which but as I passed one of the high oak doors I heard Uncle Vincent's voice coming from the room inside.

"It would probably be the best way," he was saying. "It is not the sort of thing that I would approve of normally but under the circumstances . . ."

"I will be very careful." It was Fergus's voice that replied. "They will not know a thing."

41

"I have every trust in you," Uncle Vincent said and I heard chairs being drawn back and footsteps coming towards the door. "I shall leave it all to you."

Terrified that I might be seen, I dashed down the hall to a high wooden chest and cowered down behind it.

Uncle Vincent and Fergus came out into the hall, their heads bowed and their hands clasped behind their backs. Still talking to one another, they walked away in the opposite direction from where I crouched, shuddering and afraid.

Once they were out of sight I sprang up, bounded upstairs and along the passage to our bedroom. I wrenched the door open, shut it behind myself and stood with my back to it, the palms of my hands spread out against it. The thumping of my heart raced my blood through my body and Fergus's words echoed through my head, "They will not know a thing." For minutes I stood listening, intent with fear, but I heard nothing. There was no sound in the night. Only Sara's regular breathing as she slept with her head pillowed on her arm.

At last I crept across the room and into bed, where I lay in a tight, tense ball. I told myself not to be so silly, that this was the twentieth century and that I could get away from Deersmalen whenever I liked. All I had to do was pack my case, walk to Gartleven early next morning, catch the train from there and I could be home before night. I had my return ticket, the money Daddy had given me in case of emergencies, and there were plenty of our friends at home who would let me stay with them until Mummy and Daddy came back.

I was just about to get out of bed and pack my case when common sense returned to me. Sara had been staying at Deersmalen for as long as I had and how she would laugh, I thought, if she knew that I suspected Uncle Vincent and Fergus of trying to harm us. Probably they hadn't even been talking about us.

I lay flat on my back and gazed up at the intricate plaster-work of the ceiling. What I had to do was to solve the mystery and not go running away with my tail between my legs. Gradually I drifted into sleep. The last thing I heard before I lost consciousness was the long-drawn, melancholy cry of one of Fergus's grey dogs.

I woke to daylight and the sound of rain. Running to the window I looked out. Mist wreathed the pines, the sky was leaden grey and the rain fell in spiking sheets of water. The ponies had come down from the hill and were standing under the trees. There were only four of them. The white Polly and the dun Turk were missing. Perhaps Uncle Vincent and Fergus were planning to start today hoping that Edgar would stay behind.

I was right. When I opened the kitchen door Jamie shouted, "We're starting today. Fergus is ready. He's loading the ponies and we're to be at the stables by ten if we're going."

"If we're going!" I said scornfully. "Of course we're going."

"That's what I said too," Edgar told me. "As if a drop of rain would stop us."

"We'll lend you oilskins," Aunt Sadie said. "They're the only thing for weather like this."

We were ready and waiting by ten o'clock. Jamie, Shona, Edgar and myself, four assorted bundles of oilskins, sou'-westers and wellington boots.

"You are ready then?" Fergus asked, appearing from one of the doorways, his grey dogs at his heels. He too was cocooned in oilskin. His collar turned up to meet the brim of his sou'wester so that only his bright eyes glittered from the gloom. He led Polly out. She was heavily loaded and her pack covered with oilskin.

Uncle Vincent came striding towards us down the path from the house. His black, rain-gleaming oilskin crackled and flapped about him, his great, black beard was diamonded with raindrops, the bone in his nose strained whitely through his tanned skin and his hand, powerful and claw-like, its weatherbeaten skin darkened by the rain, gripped the ram's horn handle of his crommach.

43

Our leader had arrived. He took Polly's halter rope and held her while Fergus brought out Turk, also laden with an oilskin-covered pack.

"You are ready?" Uncle Vincent demanded, looking about him. "Then let us start."

It was a nightmare journey. The rain never stopped. It beat ferociously against us, stinging into our faces, burning our bare hands and trickling down our necks in freezing rivulets. I slipped into a bog and filled one of my wellingtons with icy sludge. On and on we went, Uncle Vincent, Fergus, the grey dogs, Polly and Turk, ever before us. Long ago the Highland people must have journeyed like this, walking over the same moorland as I struggled over now, before them their chieftain and his wise man, about them their shaggy, native ponies and their hunting dogs. The same rain must have numbed their senses, the same mists wreathed about them. My legs moved automatically. My eyes were fixed on the ponies' rounded rumps. Their black skins showed through their soaked hair and the rain streamed off their long tails.

About midday we stopped and ate chocolate and biscuits, while Polly and Turk munched oats. Then on we went again. We never saw a road and there was hardly any sign of habitation. Now and again a whitewashed cottage would loom out of the mists that lay low over the hills and once a black-and-white collie trailed us a little way, yapping suspiciously. But that was all. There was nothing but endless grey-green hills, rain and mist.

Jamie and Shona marched silently ahead of me. Only Edgar, trotting at my side, breathless and soaking, spoke. He was fiddling with his compass and trying to cheer himself up with the thought of how he would retail his adventures in front of the common-room fire. For once I was glad of his company. He was the only one besides myself who seemed to notice the rain. It looked as if Shona and Jamie, Uncle Vincent and Fergus might go on for ever over the very edge of the world.

44

It was after four when Uncle Vincent stopped and waited for us to catch up with him.

"It is not a night for sleeping in the open," Uncle Vincent said. "If we go on for another two miles there is a cave where we can spend the night."

"That would be super," Edgar enthused.

Jamie, Shona and I stood dumbly waiting. I was too cold and too tired to care what we did next. Where Uncle Vincent and Fergus went I would follow.

"Right," Jamie said. "Lead the way."

The entrance to the cave was a small dark hole in the hillside. Uncle Vincent took a torch from his pocket. "I shall go first," he said, "and light the way. When you are all in, Fergus can unload the ponies and pass the loads down to us."

Uncle Vincent switched on the torch and crawled into the cave. We followed him in one by one. Once through the entrance, the tunnel became much higher so that we could almost stand upright. Ahead of me I could just make out the thin beam of the torch.

"I've reached the cave." The deep voice of Uncle Vincent came to us from the dark. "The rest of you stay in the tunnel and pass down the things to me."

"O.K.," Shona replied from behind me. "I'll tell Fergus we're ready."

The ponies' packs were in four large bundles which we passed from one to the other.

"That's the last," Shona yelled. "We can all go down now."

The cave was as large as our small bedroom at home. The floor was dry and sandy, marked in the centre with blackened rings from past fires. Uncle Vincent shone the feeble pencil beam of the torch about him in the darkness.

"You can hardly see the top of it," Jamie said. "We've never been here before, have we, Shona?"

"Not this one," Shona agreed. "Honestly, you're just beginning to think that you know all the places that Fergus and Dad know and then quite casually they produce a place like this."

"If you think you will ever know all the places Fergus and I know you are foolisher than I thought you were," Uncle Vincent said, laughing to himself.

While we shed our oilskins and sou'westers, Uncle Vincent brought dry branches from the back of the cave and lit a fire. He struck a match and put it to a heap of dry leaves. The flame soared to instant life, catching greedily at the twigs which he fed to it. Carefully he laid the branches over the flames until the fire had a glowing heart to it and the flames leapt and danced, casting fantastic shadows on the walls of the cave.

After we had eaten our supper, prepared by Fergus and Shona, of corned beef, bread and butter and a steaming mugful of tomato soup heated in the tin, we sat in a circle around the fire, warm, full and contented.

"I wish ponies were more domesticated," Shona said wistfully. "It would be gorgeous if Polly and Turk could come in and sleep by the fire like the Grey Ones, instead of having to stay out in all that rain."

"Did you hobble them?" Uncle Vincent asked Fergus.

"No," Fergus said. "I left them loose. They will find a sheltered place for themselves and come back to us in the morning."

Edgar, sitting beside me, had been strangely quiet and I turned to him to see what he was doing. He was writing in one of the notebooks which he always carried with him.

"What are you doing?" I asked him.

"Trying to remember my compass readings," he told me. "You see, if I write them all down I can look them up on a map afterwards and work out where we've been."

I glanced up at Uncle Vincent but he was still talking to Fergus about the ponies. "If I were you," I muttered to Edgar, "I wouldn't tell Uncle Vincent that that's what you're doing."

"Why on earth not?" Edgar demanded.

"Well, I don't think he'd be at all pleased."

"As if I care whether he's pleased or not. If it hadn't been for Aunt Sadie he would never have let me come with you. To tell you the truth, I don't much care for Uncle Vincent or for Fergus."

"What are you two muttering about?" Shona asked us.

"Nothing," I replied hurriedly. "I was just . . ."

"Well, we're going to sing," she interrupted me.

Even as Shona spoke, the strong, deep voice of Uncle Vincent rose and soared above us. His singing was relaxed and easy and as he sang the expression on his face which was normally stern and forbidding lifted and became gentler, more kindly. His grey eyes smiled from under his black brows and his lips curved as he sang. It was as if for a little while he had put aside the burden which Deersmalen laid upon him and in the warm, firelit security of the cave he was at peace, no longer a man alone, set apart from others by his responsibilities but a man at one with his children, his trusted servant and his niece whose face was cast in the same mould as his own.

We all joined in as he sang "Westering Home," "The Skye Boat Song," "The Rowan Tree," "Will Ye No Come Back Again," "The Kerry Dancers" and "The Old House".

Then Fergus, flanked on either side by his grey dogs, his eyes gazing into the flames, his pony hands with their long, brittle-looking fingers clasped around his knees, sang alone in Gaelic. Songs of the lonely islands and the long waiting for the loved one who does not return; songs of the spring, bringing new life and hope; songs of the first snows of the winter bringing death to the old and hunger to the young; songs of the Highland spirit haunted by the glimmerings of Tir nan Og and songs of the clans' battles and the long, bitter weariness of the clearances.

But suddenly Fergus's singing changed. The words were gone and only the music remained. "Get you up and dance," he shouted and even if he hadn't spoken I couldn't have stayed still while his wild mouth music swirled about the cave.

Jamie grabbed me by the hand and pulled me to my feet

and we were dancing. Fergus took his silver pipe from his belt and setting it to his lips he played whilst Jamie and I, Shona and Edgar, twisted and stamped, clapped our hands and sprang into the air like dervishes. My feet were possessed by Fergus's piping. Only Uncle Vincent stayed still, smiling up at us as we danced puppet-like to the strains of Fergus's music. At last Fergus stopped and we flung ourselves down on the floor of the cave, exhausted.

"And do you know, I can't dance a step really," Edgar panted.

"Some day," Shona said, gasping for breath, "you'll kill me, Fergus. You'll go on and on piping and I'll go on and on dancing until I drop dead."

"Ah ha! I can still make you dance. That warms the blood and makes the heart beat stronger," Fergus crowed. "Only the Master can withstand the music of Fergus's pipe."

We sat on for a while by the fire, drinking cocoa made from dried milk and water. Then we unpacked our sleeping bags, Uncle Vincent put more wood on the fire, and with our feet to the blaze we slept.

Next day the sun was shining, white clouds scudded over a pale blue sky and larks burst from the heather, throwing themselves upwards in ecstasy. We packed our oilskins on to the ponies' backs and our journeying was happy and simple. Fergus walked with us, telling us tales of the wild life of the Highlands, while Uncle Vincent, a pony at his either side, strode on ahead, alone.

Lunch was long and leisurely with everyone taking their time and basking in the sun. Even Polly tried to lie down and roll but was stopped just in time by Jamie.

After lunch the land we travelled over became more rugged, great boulders bright with yellow tormentil and lichens, lay strewn amongst the heather. We followed a sheep track down the mountainside and then made our way along the bottom of a gorge. As we went along, the mountains seemed to close in until all the sky that was left to us was a twisting ribbon of blue high above our heads. We were almost entombed in a tunnel of black rock. Yet, strangely, the tempo of our journey became faster and faster. I could feel the suppressed excitement in Jamie, Shona and Fergus and even in Uncle Vincent. I glanced at Edgar, wondering if he felt it, but he was looking at his compass and didn't seem to notice. Once Fergus pointed to a black speck in the sky and said, "Golden eagle," but it could have been anything, it was so high and remote.

Jamie, as if he could stand the strain no longer, flipped on to his hands and with a swift succession of cartwheels was alongside his father.

"We're nearly there," he said, springing upright.

Uncle Vincent glanced quickly back at us then nodded his head.

Our track led upwards now, climbing out of the gorge. Then it twisted sharply right and dropped down to the shores of a small loch. The water of the loch was black and dark as night, mirroring the black rocks that sloped steeply down towards it. There was no breath of life about it. No birds sang, few plants grew on its shores, all was bleak and desolate. On three sides its waters lapped against the black rocks but the fourth was a barren shore that became grey-green bog land and stretched away in forsaken marsh.

"We will make our camp here," Uncle Vincent said, halting Polly and Turk.

"Oh, not here," I exclaimed. "No one would want to spend the night here. Oh, do let's go on a bit. It's horrible here."

"Don't be daft, Kay," Jamie said vehemently. "I would live here for ever if I could. Out of all Scotland this is my bit of land. I belong here."

"Perhaps Kay is right. It is not as if we were alone. We shall go on a little way before we stop," Uncle Vincent decided.

"It would be as well," said Fergus.

"Why?" demanded Shona. "Why can't we stay here, why?"

Her father didn't answer her, but taking up the ponies' halter ropes again he led the way on over the marsh.

We had three small tents with us, one for Shona and me, one for Uncle Vincent and Fergus, and one for Edgar and Jamie. When Uncle Vincent stopped and Fergus unloaded the ponies, Jamie and Edgar pitched the tents on a hillock of dry land rising from the marshier ground.

"It doesn't seem a very good place to me," I grumbled. We could still see the midnight waters of the loch and its chill dread still seemed to be all around us. "Couldn't we have gone on out of sight of the loch?" I pleaded, but no one took any notice of me.

Fergus finished unloading Polly and Turk, but, unlike last night, after he had watered and fed them he tethered them to two stunted rowan trees which were growing close by. Jamie and Shona laid the sleeping bags out on top of the ground sheets in the tents and then they went off together to get water from a spring at the lochside. Uncle Vincent had lit a fire with dry tinder wood which he had brought from the cave and when it was burning red we cooked sausages over it and ate them with bread and butter. As we sat around the fire the light gradually faded from the sky and the grey, cold dusk covered the marshland, the black mountains and the unfathomable depths of the loch.

"We will not bother with more wood for the fire," Uncle Vincent said when Edgar offered to go and look for some. "The night is not cold. Fergus shall tell us a story and then we shall sleep for we have a long day ahead of us tomorrow. We shall travel back to Deersmalen in the one day. I have been away long enough."

Fergus settled himself more comfortably on the ground and began his tale of how he had lived a whole year with a herd of red deer, moving when they moved, living as they lived, so that he might learn their ways.

But I was the only one who really listened to him. Edgar was too busy writing down his compass bearings in his notebook to pay much attention, Uncle Vincent was gazing out over our heads to the black sheen of the loch's water and it was quite obvious that Shona and Jamie could hardly sit still for excitement. The secret of the journey is going to happen tonight, I told myself. Whatever happens I must keep close to Shona. If I have to I'll stay awake all night, I thought, and I felt brave and excited.

Fergus finished his story. "And yet," he concluded, "I know but little of the deer. I did not become one of them although I lived with them, for I watched them with human eyes and a human brain told me what I saw. Now I will make cocoa for us and then we shall all be sleeping."

Fergus mixed water and dried milk, boiled it over the fire, then pouring it into mugs he added sugar and cocoa and handed us a mug each.

"I'm going to drink mine in my tent," Shona said, picking her cocoa up and taking it into our tent. "Goodnight."

"I'm coming too," I muttered, and carefully carrying my mug of steaming cocoa I said goodnight and crawled after Shona into the tiny space of the tent. I heard Jamie and Edgar say goodnight to Uncle Vincent and Fergus and go into their tent.

Sitting down on top of my sleeping bag I pulled off my wellingtons. I tucked my feet underneath me and sipped my cocoa. The hot liquid glowed warmly through me. I held the mug in both hands and drank it slowly.

"Was it true?" I asked Shona. "All that Fergus was telling us about living with the deer?"

"Of course," Shona answered. "Everything Fergus tells you is true."

"Why are you staring at me like that?" I asked her. "I bet I don't look any muckier than you do."

"No," said Shona and giggled.

"Don't giggle at me like that," I said peevishly, but suddenly I was too sleepy to care. My eyelids fell like weighted lead over my eyes. My whole body ached with an undeniable desire for sleep. "Gosh I'm sleepy," I yawned.

"Are you?" said Shona's laughing voice.

"Terribly."

"You should just get into your sleeping bag the way you are," Shona said, and taking my empty mug from me she helped me into the warm closeness of my sleeping bag.

"Thanks," I murmured, already half asleep. For a second my mind struggled to regain a lost idea, a mystery that I would solve tonight if I could only stay with Shona. But it was too late and my eyes closed against my will.

CHAPTER FOUR

"Kay, wake up. Wake up, Kay." I heard the irritating nag of Edgar's voice reaching me from a long way off, prying me from my limpet shell of sleep. "Wake up, Kay. We'll be too late if you don't get up now."

Slowly my mind struggled towards him. "What d'you want?" I muttered sleepily. "Go away and leave me alone."

"If you don't come now we'll be too far behind to follow them," Edgar told me frantically. "Jamie, Shona, Fergus and Uncle Vincent have taken Polly and they're all going somewhere. And if you won't get up I'm going after them myself."

Edgar's last words banished my longing for sleep. I sat up awake at last. "I knew they'd go somewhere tonight," I said.

"Well you were right. Buck up and put your boots on or we'll be too late."

Obediently I struggled into my wellingtons and followed Edgar out. We crouched at the side of the tent looking about us in the pale moonlight.

"There they are," Edgar whispered. "They're going to the loch. I was jolly sure they would. I knew there was something queer about it when we passed it this afternoon."

I nodded, agreeing with him. The night air was chilly and I shuddered as a goose walked over my grave. Suddenly I wished that Edgar hadn't woken me up. I longed to be back in the safe warmth of my sleeping bag.

"Do you think we should follow them?" I asked doubtfully. "I don't think Uncle Vincent can want us to see what they're doing."

"Uncle Vincent *want* us to see," Edgar echoed in astonishment. "Of course he doesn't want us to see. Don't tell me that you haven't realised that you were drugged?"

"No," I said sheepishly.

"Well you were," Edgar told me. "We both should have been, only I was on the lookout. Just like a girl not to notice there was something fishy going on. I guessed Fergus had put something in the cocoa so I poured it out when Jamie wasn't looking and just pretended to be asleep."

"That means," I said, "that they definitely don't want us to see them."

"All the more reason why we should go and find out. If you ask me they're up to no good. Come on, we'll need to hurry."

"Honestly, Edgar," I protested, "I don't think we should."

"No one's going to try and dope me and get away with it," Edgar stated. "I'm going after them. You can do what you like." And he began to walk over the marsh towards the loch.

For a second I hesitated. Part of me knew that I had no right to spy on Uncle Vincent, that their midnight journey to the loch was not meant for our eyes. But even as I hesitated, curiosity got the better of me. "He'd no right to dope me," I thought indignantly. "Serve them right if we follow them." And I scuttled after Edgar.

We crept, one behind the other, over the marshy ground until we reached a huge boulder close to the shore of the loch.

"This should do us," Edgar said, peering round the edge of it. "You can see all the shore. They're down there now. Look."

Cautiously I looked. Shona and Jamie were holding Polly, and Uncle Vincent and Fergus were standing a little way apart, talking together. Fergus's two great dogs stood by them, ears pricked, bodies alert. The full moon sailed free in a cloudless sky, lighting the black swoop of the rocks down to the silent depths of the loch. An icy wind blew from the water, stirring the marsh reeds and lifting strands of Shona's silvery hair about her shoulders.

"They don't seem to be doing anything much," I whispered to Edgar.

55

"Not yet," he agreed and we cowered down for warmth behind our boulder.

"I wonder how long they'll be. It's bitter out here, isn't it?" I said.

Edgar nodded and stood up again to look at the loch. "Hey," he said. "They're doing something now."

I stood up to see and what I saw made my blood run cold. Fergus, a grey dog on either side of him, was standing alone facing the loch. In his hand, glinting in the moonlight, was his pipe. Uncle Vincent stood just behind him staring out over the water.

Even as I watched, Fergus set his pipe to his lips and the first high, haunting notes escaped into the night. If he had called the seals in from the sea what would his music conjure into being from the black dread of the loch?

I seized Edgar by the arm. "Let's go back to the tents," I pleaded. "Now, before it's too late. Please, Edgar."

Edgar stared at me in astonishment. "Not bloomin' likely," he said. "Go back yourself if you want to. This is just getting interesting."

The music of Fergus, high and haunting, low and be-seeching, was all about us. I had never heard him play his pipe like this before. The being he called from the dark waters was no beast being ordered to slaughter like the seals, or an equal, as we had been when he piped for our dancing. This music was low and reverent, it spoke of willing service continuing from generation to generation, of lives gladly sacrificed. It pleaded with that which was hidden to reveal itself.

As Fergus played, ringing ripples stirred the quicksilver surface of the loch. Gradually the commotion of the water became more and more violent. Like some vast cauldron, the water boiled and frothed. Then, from the midst of the confusion, a black head appeared, and plunging upward to the shallower water at the loch's edge came an immense black horse.

I shall never forget my first sight of the Water Horse as it rose from the darkness of the loch into the moon-silvered shallows. The water poured from its long mane and streaming tail. Its bulging shoulders and great muscled quarters were sleeked and gleaming. Its neck, arched like the necks of the horses on a Greek frieze, held aloft in the moonlight a head of exquisite breeding, a network of veins beneath a

satin-fine skin, eyes large, liquid-soft and glistening, and scarlet nostrils flaunting the night for danger. The great Horse moved through the water, spurning it into sparkling drops with its flying hoofs and I held my arm over my eyes for fear and awe at the sight. It was a being from a lost age, proud, powerful and alien to the petty confusion of our living.

"Cor!" exclaimed Edgar. "He's an absolute whopper, isn't he?" and the inadequacy of his words jangled my tightly-strained nerves.

"Shut up," I whispered hoarsely.

The Horse came stepping out of the water, lifting his feet high. Its tail, carried like an Arab's, streamed out behind it. Once it reached dry land it whinnied with a noise like thunder, reared up and was away, galloping in a huge circle over the marsh and back to Uncle Vincent and Fergus.

It was only when the Horse stood beside Uncle Vincent that I realised just how high it was. Uncle Vincent, who was taller than most men, barely reached to its shoulder. I watched entranced as he held out his hand to the Horse. It stretched its neck and blew softly over his arm. Uncle Vincent stood perfectly still, talking gently to the Horse. Then he moved quietly forward until he could run his hand along the Horse's neck.

The Horse stood like a graven image with Uncle Vincent at its head, while Fergus, quick and confident as a professional groom, moved about it. From where I watched I could see Uncle Vincent's lips and knew he was talking to it all the time. When Fergus had finished looking the Water Horse over he joined Uncle Vincent at its head and they stood together for a long time, the Horse's head resting on Uncle Vincent's shoulder, relaxed and at peace.

Watching them, I longed to be able to walk across the shore and stand close to the Horse. Just to stand and fill my vision with its beauty was all I asked of life. I knew now why Jamie had said he would choose to live by the Black Loch. It would be like living close to a God and never knowing when your day would be charged with joy by the sight of Him.

"Do you think we should go back now?" Edgar asked. "We want to get back to the tents before Uncle Vincent and Fergus."

I knew he was right but I desperately wanted to stay and watch the Water Horse for as long as I possibly could.

"Do we need to go now?" I whispered. "Let's stay just a bit longer."

"There'll be a terrible blow-up if we're not back before them. Come on, we'd better go. We've seen all there is to see anyway."

I took one long last look at Uncle Vincent, Fergus and the Water Horse and even as I stared the Horse lifted up its head from Uncle Vincent's shoulder and turned back to the loch.

"That's it going back," Edgar said. "We'll need to dash. Goodness knows what they would do if they found out that we'd been watching them. Not that I care, mind you."

Together we hurried back to the tents.

"I'm jolly glad we went," Edgar said as we stumbled along over the tufted reeds. "I'd never have believed it if I hadn't seen it with my own eyes."

"It was the most wonderful thing I've ever seen in my whole life," I said.

"Yes," said Edgar. "It was smashing. Just imagine the money a zoo would pay for it. Or a scientist, to be able to discover how it breathes underwater. Bet you they'd pay thousands and thousands."

"Whatever do you mean?" I gasped in horror. "Fancy even thinking of that!"

"Well, why not? It would be frightfully interesting to see it properly and find out all about it. I suppose all you'd want to do is to sit and stare at it and say, 'Oh how beautiful!' all the time," Edgar said scornfully. I didn't answer him, but with a cold, sinking feeling in the pit of my stomach I wondered if Uncle Vincent had been right. If it would have been better if Edgar and I had stayed asleep and unsuspecting in our tents.

We had almost reached the tents when Edgar exclaimed, "I say, look, Fergus's dogs have got there before us."

I looked at the tents more carefully and saw in front of each of them a long, lean, grey shape. "That's queer," I said. "Surely they were still with Fergus when we left them."

59

"Well, they're here now," Edgar said. "Perhaps he sent them on ahead."

"We never saw them pass us," I said. "We'll need to get them to move before we can get into our tents."

"Oh, I'll soon shift them," Edgar declared confidently, and stepping up to the dog that lay in front of his tent he held out his hand to it.

"Come on, old boy," Edgar said. "Out of the way and let me in."

The dog lifted its head from its paws and wrinkling back its lips showed curving yellow fangs. It snarled from the depths of its throat and its tawny eyes glowed in the dark.

Edgar leapt back in fright : "Can't be used to strangers," he muttered, standing well away from the dog. "You try, Kay."

"Me?" I said. "What makes you think it would like me any better? It looks to me as if it hated everyone."

Edgar regarded the dog apprehensively "Try the other one," he suggested. "Maybe it'll be better-natured.'

I went across to my tent but as soon as I got within yards of the opening the dog sprang to its feet and with its neck thrust out, head lowered, it glared balefully up at me.

"What's the matter?" I asked it, in what I hoped were soothing tones. "Nobody's going to touch you. I just want to get into my tent."

As I spoke I stepped towards the dog. It curled its lips back, snarling evilly, the hackles on its neck standing up-right. I held my hand out to it and quicker than sight it lunged forward, slashing with its teeth at my arm. I sprang back and its teeth snapped together, missing my arm by inches.

"Leave it alone, Kay," Edgar shouted, but I had no intention of doing anything else. I hurried back to where Edgar stood.

"We'll never get past them," I said. "That one really tried to bite me."

"We must be back in our sleeping bags before Uncle Vincent gets here," Edgar said. "If even one of us could get back in, the other could say they'd heard the dogs and come out to see what was happening. You wouldn't like to see if you could get them both over to your tent while I try to get into mine?"

"Not likely," I said. "I don't fancy being a human sacrifice, thank you very much."

We both stood staring at the dogs.

"There must be some way,' Edgar said, beginning to panic. "We *must* be in our tents before Uncle Vincent catches us. Not that I'm scared of him but just imagine all the fuss there'd be."

While Edgar was talking I suddenly realised what it was that was so uncanny about Fergus's dogs.

"Do you remember that book you won as a form prize?" I asked Edgar. "The one about Russian heroes. You had it on holiday with you one year."

" 'Course I remember it," Edgar said irritably. "What on earth has that to do with us just now?"

"Remember the way the illustrations looked like photographs, they were so real?"

Edgar nodded. "So what?" he said.

"Well, you know the picture of Petrov holding the wolves at bay while the rest of them escaped?"

I didn't need to explain any more. I saw the blood drain from Edgar's face, leaving it chalky white in the moonlight.

"Don't talk nonsense, Kay," he said loudly, trying to bluff himself. "There haven't been any wolves in Scotland for centuries." But his voice trailed away lamely as he looked down at Fergus's grey dogs. "They couldn't possibly . . ."

"But they are," I said with conviction. "Jamie and Shona never call them dogs, always the Grey Ones, and that's what they are, they're wolves."

As if to confirm what I had just said, the wolf in front of Edgar's tent sat up on its haunches, and, pointing its muzzle to the sky, it howled a long vibrating note into the night.

"We'll never get past them now," Edgar whined. "And it'll be worse for me. They hate me. They could do anything to us here and nobody would ever know. There's nothing Fergus wouldn't do if Uncle Vincent told him to. Look at the way he doped us. He might even murder us and say we'd fallen off a cliff or stepped into a bog or anything. He might even feed us to his wolves!"

"Don't be an idiot, Edgar. You're only making things worse, talking rubbish like that. How I wish I'd never come with you. If only you'd drunk your cocoa all this would never have happened."

"Listen," Edgar squeaked. "What's that?"

We turned to look back towards the loch and saw the dim, mothy whiteness of Polly with Uncle Vincent, Fergus, Shona and Jamie, dark shapes, walking along beside her.

"It's them," I said and we stood like trapped animals awaiting our doom.

"He's just a silly old man," Edgar muttered, more to

himself than to me. "And I couldn't care less what he says. If he does anything to me, my father . . ."

They came steadily towards us. Fergus handed Polly's rope to Shona who took her to the rowan tree and tied her up again. Then they came on until they stood in front of Edgar and myself. I couldn't look at them for shame. There was a long, heavy silence while Uncle Vincent looked down at us. At last he spoke.

"You do not need to tell me," he said. "Your guilt is written on your faces. This has been a bad night for us all. There are many to blame for it but that is little use now the damage is done. I should not have brought the boy."

I heard Edgar mutter something that sounded like, "That's right, make it all my fault," but Uncle Vincent didn't pause to listen.

"I should have taken greater care myself. The Grey Ones should have been left behind to guard you even although I was sure that you must sleep till day. And you, Kay Innes, you are to blame more than anyone else."

"Why?" I gasped, shocked by the unfairness of his words. "It was Edgar who woke me."

"You with the Innes face and the black hair must surely have known how wrong it was to spy upon hidden things. When you heard the first notes of Fergus's pipe the very blood in your veins must have cried out to you that what was to follow was no sight for Edgar's eyes."

I could think of nothing to say. I wanted to tell Uncle Vincent that I honestly hadn't understood about Edgar. That it wasn't until Edgar had said that scientists or a zoo would pay thousands for the Water Horse that I had realised the evil Edgar might do. I truly hadn't known that anyone could see a creature as majestic as the Water Horse and think of it only in terms of money or science. But I couldn't find words to say these things. "I'm sorry," I mumbled.

"So was Eve after she had tasted the apple. How sorry we all are when we discover that the fruit is bitter but then it is always too late and the price must be paid. And as for you, Edgar, there is little I can say to you except to ask you

63

to forget all you have seen tonight, to put it from your mind, not even to think of it. That is the one way for your future happiness. Your life should not have crossed such dark ways as these. Remember tonight and your whole life will be shadowed by what you have seen yet will never understand."

I glanced at Edgar from the corner of my eye. He was fiddling with a piece of string, running it through his fingers, knotting and unknotting it, and now that he realised that Uncle Vincent wasn't going to do anything desperate to us Edgar hardly seemed to be listening to him.

"How did Fergus know to send his wolves back for us?" Edgar demanded in a sulky voice when Uncle Vincent paused.

"Ah, so you have discovered that too," Fergus said, "Now that you know, it is our courtesy to call them Grey Ones."

"They are wolves then," breathed Edgar. "And Kay was right. There was one with you when you met us at the station and you sent it home alone because it was a wolf."

"I had a sudden suspicion that all was not well with you," continued Fergus. "I sent the Grey Ones back in case you were in need of protection. But as you know that was not so."

"You needn't have bothered yourself," Edgar muttered under his breath.

Uncle Vincent looked at him as if he could see into his very soul. "Do you think, boy, that I do not know what I am talking about? All I have said tonight is the truth. You would do well to heed it. Now go to your tent and stay there until the morning. You have done enough harm for one night."

Edgar turned and walked slowly over to his tent, stooped and crawled inside. At a sign from Fergus, one of the Grey Ones crossed and lay down at the tent's opening.

Uncle Vincent turned to me and spoke. "When I first planned this journey," he said, "I intended to show you to the Water Horse, but when Edgar was included in the

64

party I changed my mind, thinking it better that you should both be left in your tents. But now that you have seen the Horse we must go back to the loch tonight and discover if the Horse will acknowledge you as its future guardian."

I heard Jamie gasp, and when I turned his face was peaked and strained under the pale wing of his hair. His father gripped Jamie's shoulder with one of his strong hands and spoke gently to him. "If this thing is to be it is better that we should all face it. There is no peace to be found for any of us in a world of make-believe and dreams." Jamie nodded slowly. "If Kay is the chosen one it is better that we should know now," continued Uncle Vincent. "Shona, stay here with your brother. Fergus and I will go with Kay."

As I stood on the loch shore listening again to the high, sweet piping of Fergus, I was filled with a joyful expectancy, as if this were the thing for which I had been waiting all my life. Beneath my feet, the shingle oozed clear water, and high, high above me was the infinity of space cradling in its void the round, cold fish of the moon.

"You are not afraid?"

I looked up at Uncle Vincent and shook my head for I I knew no fear, only a gladness more awe-inspiring than anything I had experienced in my life before.

Again the Horse broke the sheet silver of the loch's surface and came towards us, dark against the path of the moon's reflection. I saw it now in detail which I had been unable to see before; the delicate curve of its ears, carven and hollow as shells; the whorled cavity of its nostrils drawn back as it sensed a stranger; the strong, flat bones at cheek and knee and the fall of mane diamonded with sparkling water drops.

Slowly the Horse came towards us—its head outstretched, its neck arched. It reached the loch's edge and stood poised between the slight forward movement which would show its trust in me and the violent swerve on its haunches that would carry it back, bursting and threshing through the icy waters to the security of its underwater world.

C

Uncle Vincent laid his arm on my shoulders. "This is Kay of Innes," he said in a voice low and soft, so that the words were more imagined than heard.

At his voice the Horse relaxed and with its liquid eyes doe-gentle it came out of the froth-frilled shallows and stood by us. I lifted my hand and ran it down the hard muscled neck of the Horse. It nickered with a tremor of sound and did not move away from my touch.

It stayed only a little while, then turned and went from us, stepping delicately through the cold white fire of the loch's water, withdrawing its presence as a god. We watched in silence until the surface of the loch lay still and untroubled under the night.

"It is Kay. She is the chosen one," Uncle Vincent said as Jamie started to his feet at our approach. As we had walked back from the loch Uncle Vincent had explained that while he lived he was the guardian of the Water Horse and that it was not until his death that I would take his place. I walked at his side, seeing nothing of my surroundings, my mind's eye still filled with the beauty of the Horse.

Only for a second Jamie paused, biting back his bitter disappointment. "All my life I shall serve you and the Water Horse," he said to me. "I am glad that I shall have this honour." And he turned away towards his tent.

I slept deeply, but when I woke to the grey stillness before dawn all the night's happenings were vividly before me and my heart sang with joy and pride at the memory of the Horse and my future guardianship.

After a cold breakfast of stalish bread and meat paste, we loaded Polly and Turk and set out for Deersmalen.

We went back the way we had come; passing the loch, lying cold and unearthly in the early light, on and through the gorge, over the rough moorland and back to the rolling hills which we had crossed on our first day's journey. Edgar walked behind, speaking to no one, and I too walked silently, slowly realising the terrible thing I had done when I had allowed Edgar to spy on the Water Horse.

We reached Deersmalen as the first stars began to speckle the sky.

"You will not speak to anyone of what you have seen," Uncle Vincent cautioned us. "I will see you in my study tomorrow morning after breakfast."

Aunt Sadie had a meal waiting for us which we ate and then staggered upstairs to fall exhausted into our beds.

Next morning after breakfast Jamie knocked on the door of his father's study.

"Come in," Uncle Vincent shouted, and we all trooped in and stood in a semi-circle round the heavy oak desk at which Uncle Vincent was seated.

"I asked you to come here this morning so that I could tell you something about the Innes family and about the Horse which you all saw at the Black Loch. Also to ask Edgar to give me his solemn promise that he will never mention the Horse to any other living soul."

"Why me?" demanded Edgar.

"It is with you that the danger lies. Kay will not speak of it. Fergus thinks that you should be sent home but I do not like that idea nor does your aunt. If you, Edgar, wish to tell the world of the existence of the Water Horse you will do so no matter where you are."

"Huh!" said Edgar.

"Now I will tell you a little about your family history. You are, as you know, Inneses of Deersmalen, as your fathers are and their father was before them."

He was speaking now especially to Edgar and me and I supposed that Jamie and Shona knew what he was about to tell us.

"The Innes family have lived here since the fourteenth century and maybe before that. I know from written evidence of that time that even then there was a Water Horse in the Black Loch and that it was the duty of the House of Innes to tend and protect it. It is a duty which is still ours today. From my generation I was the chosen one. Your fathers had also seen the Horse but they did not wish to stay at Deersmalen and when they told me that they were

67

going to leave I was filled with an unreasoning fear that they would talk carelessly about the Horse and in some way its secret would be disclosed. We fought violently and for many years after their going I heard no word of them. Your father, Edgar, is my elder brother and he came back once to sign legal papers which required his signature. Ten years ago, Kay, your father wrote to me telling me of your strong resemblance to the Innes family. Since then he has done a great deal to make it possible for me to stay at Deersmalen close to the Horse. And now with your coming I hope that the stupid quarrel may be ended. A stupid quarrel because your fathers have never breathed a word about the Horse.

"My wife and Caroline know of the existence of the Horse but have never seen it. Many of the crofters know of it as a legend but they do not know which loch it inhabits. Once, twelve years ago, a child and her uncle who were camping close to the loch saw the Horse grazing by the loch-side. It was evening, the grey dusk between day and night, and the man dismissed what he had seen as an optical illusion but the child remembers to this day what she saw but fortunately does not know which loch she was at when she saw it. For a long time after this we were afraid that someone would listen to the girl's story but nobody believed her and now I think the danger is past.

"I had hoped that in the next generation the stewardship of the Water Horse would have passed to my son. But Kay has the family features and the honour has fallen to her. I have great faith in you, Kay."

"But what good does it do?" Edgar asked suddenly. "Whopping great horse like that stuck away in a loch where nobody can see it. I think it would be miles better in a zoo or a museum where everyone could benefit from it."

There was a deadly silence after Edgar's words.

For a second Uncle Vincent lowered his head on to his hands, then, looking straight at Edgar, he said, "If even after seeing the Water Horse, Edgar, you do not understand, I cannot explain. You must try to believe that a great

68

power for good comes from any creature living free and proud in its own right, that by its very existence it praises God. That in some way which even I do not fully understand the beauty and strength of the Water Horse and the long years of service given by your family atone very slightly for some of the evil of the world."

"Sounds pretty crummy to me," Edgar muttered.

"Now you must give me your solemn word that you will never tell anyone about the Water Horse. That you will never hint or joke about it, making others suspicious. That you will talk about it to no one."

"I promise," Edgar mumbled. As he spoke I heard a patter of claws on the wooden floor and I glanced behind me to see the little black dog, Merchant, trotting across the room. As I looked back at Uncle Vincent I saw that Edgar, hands behind his back, had his fingers crossed.

"Now," said Uncle Vincent, "off you go and find Caroline and Sara. They have something to tell you which should keep you occupied for a week. And remember you are all to stay together. There is to be no more going off and leaving Edgar alone."

Obediently we left the study. I considered telling Jamie that Edgar had had his fingers crossed when he had given his promise to Uncle Vincent. But on second thoughts I decided that it sounded childish and that it was probably just a coincidence.

"We'd better find Caro," Jamie said, marching down the corridor, "and discover what is going to keep us occupied for the next week."

"As if we couldn't guess," Shona glowered, striding along beside him.

CHAPTER FIVE

We found Caroline, Sara and Aunt Sadie in the kitchen.

"Well, that's it over," Shona said to her mother. "And we're to stay together in the civilised company of Sara and Caroline for one week. As you will be glad to hear," she ended, bowing to Sara and Caroline.

"You would have had to help us anyway," Caroline said. "The Reids from Craig Garth were all down here yesterday afternoon. It's dear Andrea's twenty-first birthday on Friday, so instead of having their usual dance in the middle of September they are having a great, glorious, slap-up dance on Friday."

"I knew it!" Shona exclaimed in disgust. "I honestly believe that dance is the worst thing that happens to me in the year. Here I am, leading a quiet, contented life and then—wham! I'm mixed up with a lot of ghastly county types. You should just see them, Kay. Long hair and eye shadow and high heels, and the clothes!" For a second words failed Shona. "Tweeds and little cotton dresses that probably cost a fortune and scarlet corduroy trousers with all the corduroy still on them. For a week they're everywhere, calling me Shona dear, and telling me how they just love my silver hair. Then there's the dance and that's that. You never see them again or if you do they turn up their noses at you as if you were a bad smell."

"Shona, Shona," exclaimed Aunt Sadie. "Stop talking nonsense."

"It's not nonsense. I do hate it. I hate the way they let you see all the things you haven't got. All the things I want."

"What would you do with fancy clothes or eye shadow?" demanded Aunt Sadie.

"Not just now," Shona admitted. "But some day, and

seeing them just lets me know how much I'm going to want them."

Jamie, who had been listening to her with a look of intense disgust on his face, turned away and stared out of the kitchen window.

"You see, the Reids own Craig Garth—that's the estate next to Deersmalen—but they only stay there in August and September for the shooting," Aunt Sadie explained. "They bring hordes of friends to stay with them and every year they give a dance. They haven't a hall big enough so they hold it in our dining-hall. It's like the old days in New York before I met Vin. All the excitement and the bustle. Everything money could buy for a night of laughter and fun." And seizing the protesting Edgar by the waist she whirled him around the kitchen. "How I could dance in those days. Every night, three, four, five in the morning, it made no difference to me," Aunt Sadie said, releasing Edgar. "How long ago it seems. Perhaps you are right, Shona, perhaps I hate the dance too. It reminds me of all the things that I used to have but can never have again."

"Then why do we have the beastly thing?" Jamie demanded, crashing his fist down on the draining board. "Why doesn't Dad tell them to get out of our house and stay out?"

To my amazement I thought I saw tears glistening in his eyes but he turned back to the window too quickly for me to be sure.

"Because they pay us and you know as well as I do that we need all the money we can lay our hands on to keep Deersmalen going," Aunt Sadie said, crossing over to Jamie. "We were only joking, Shona and I. Do you think I would ever dream of exchanging the things I have here, a family I love, a husband I love, land that I love, for the empty baubles which we see flaunted before us at the Craig Garth dance? Do you think that if I had wanted social position, ready money and what they call a gay life I would ever have married your father? I thought you knew me better than that, Jamie."

71

"I'm sorry, Mum," Jamie said in a choked-sounding voice.

"All the same," Edgar said, in a voice so like his father's that I could have sworn it was my Uncle James speaking, "money is a pretty good thing to have behind you. You can't get far without it, you know."

Aunt Sadie smiled pityingly at him. "You can go a long way without it and there are lots of places where money can take you that I wouldn't want to go to," she said.

"That's two of them coming up the drive now," Jamie announced. "They don't waste much time."

"Oh, it'll be Andrea and her friend. Andrea couldn't come yesterday and Mrs. Reid said she would come over this morning and bring a friend with her who is studying interior decoration. They're going to decide how they'll decorate the hall this time. Then a whole host of them are just going to crowd over on Friday morning and get to work on it. You know how too, too bright the young things are today," Aunt Sadie said.

"Don't let Andrea hear you. She'd recognise her mother," Caroline laughed.

"You go to the door," Aunt Sadie said to Caroline. "Take them to the dining-hall and let them brood in it. I must just comb my hair before they see me."

Aunt Sadie went upstairs to tidy herself up. Caroline, Edgar, Sara and Shona went to open the door and I went over to the window to have a look at Andrea and her friend.

The two girls were wearing slacks and off-the-shoulder cotton blouses. One had red hair, the other light brown, but they both had the vacant, painted faces of the girls on magazine covers.

"I've seen the red-headed one before," I said to Jamie, who was still standing staring out.

"That's Andrea," he said. "Next we have Miss Andrea Reid on her famous Flare Way. Remember now?"

"Of course, that's where I've seen her—show jumping. She jumps at all the big shows in London. I've seen her on television."

"That's right. When she was younger she used to come over here and boast and boast to us about her wonderful ponies, so we gave her a ride on one of the difficult Highlands, just bareback, the way we always ride them. She fell off at the first wall and she wouldn't get on again." Jamie giggled at the memory, his eyes bright, his nose and pointed chin becoming sharper than ever with his mirth. Once he started giggling he could never stop. He went on and on, until his laughter held him powerless in its grip. Then he gasped, choked and wiped the tears from his eyes. "I can see her yet, sitting there covered in mud. She never said another word to us about her ponies. You know something else about her," Jamie added, the laughter suddenly gone from him. "She's the girl who saw the Water Horse, the child who was camping with her uncle by the Black Loch. Once she tried to organise Shona and I into an expedition to find the loch where they had camped but of course we wouldn't go with her. She hasn't mentioned it for a long time now, perhaps she has forgotten about it. Dad seems to think so, but you never know. She had no doubts about it being a trick of the half light. She knew that she had seen a great, black horse that disappeared into the loch."

I heard the front door open and Caroline's voice welcoming them in. They all walked past the kitchen door. Andrea and her friend telling the world in general how wonderful it was to be back in Scotland and how if they had their way they would never leave it.

"I bet," Jamie said to me. "Come on, we'd better go too. You know, in a way they fascinate me. They're all so different from anyone I meet normally."

We went down the corridor and across the hall to the dining-hall.

"Do you never use it yourselves now?" I asked. "Sara told us that when she was here you had a meal in it, the grown-ups anyway."

"Must have been a special occasion," Jamie said. "We hardly ever use it now."

I followed Jamie into the dining-hall. It was a vast room.

73

Oak-panelled walls reached up to the ceiling of carved oak. Along one side of the room the curtains hung by the mullioned windows in swathes of heavy velvet. From the walls, the heads of deer and snarling fox masks, interspersed with ancient weapons, stared fixedly down at us.

"Dad and Fergus must have moved the table," Jamie said. "They have caterers up from Inverness and they have a buffet in one of the other rooms. They just dance here."

"Jamie Innes!" Andrea let out a shrill squeal and came running towards us. "I was just asking where you were. We've had the most fabulous idea for the dance. Just wait till you hear about it. And who's this? Not another cousin? I'd no idea you were so gifted with relations. You will come to my dance, won't you? It wouldn't be a dance without everyone from Deersmalen."

"This is Kay Innes," Jamie said. "Kay, meet Andrea." We shook hands and I looked curiously at this girl who by mere chance had seen the Water Horse, who held with her knowledge a threat to the Horse's life but I could see nothing beyond the mask of her conventional prettiness.

"And this," Andrea said, introducing us to her friend, "is Marjora Pilkington Waites. We just call her Pilkie. Pilkie, this is Jamie and Kay."

"How do you do," said Pilkie in one of the deepest voices I had ever heard. "Have you told them about our idea? It'll absolutely send you," she assured me, squeezing my arm.

"We're going all Scottish," Andrea told us. "Everyone will wear kilts and the girls will wear those gorgeous tartan sashes with their evening dresses. We'll look utterly ravishing and Pilkie has got some wonderful notions for decorating the place."

Jamie winced.

"Everywhere, just everywhere, tartan," Pilkie said, her voice throbbing down among her boots. "And heather. We'll cut armfuls of heather and just drown the hall in it. That purple! I've never seen anything like it in my life before."

"You can't possibly have a lot of Sassenachs dressing up in the kilt," James stated.

"Now, Jamie," Andrea said. "Don't be so prickly. But of course we can. They'll all absolutely adore it. They can hire kilts for the night."

"Just imagine Buffy's knees!" Pilkie gurgled and she and Andrea burst into rapturous giggles.

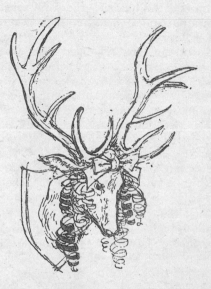

"I know, my dear, that's just it. The legs we'll see! I can't wait." Andrea sighed.

"You'd better not let Fergus hear about it," Shona said darkly.

"Oh, you wouldn't dream of telling him?" Andrea demanded, shocked. "He's the weirdest old man you ever saw," she told Pilkie. "He wanders round the hills all alone with just these two great dogs padding along beside him. He's known me ever since I was so high but I don't think he's ever said one word to me. The aura he gives off would strike you cold a mile away. You must meet him, Pilk, you absolutely must. He's just *the* cutest."

"You didn't think he was so cute the time he took down all the ribbons just before the dance," Jamie reminded her slyly.

"Don't, don't," beseeched Andrea. "How could you? D'you know I'd nearly forgotten all about it. Three years ago, it was," she told Pilkie. "Bongo Carruthers and I bought miles, but miles of ribbon and we tied it in little bows all over the heads. If you'd seen the foxes with sweet little bows on their ears and round their noses! And the deer! We tied a big ribbon round their heads and hung crêpe paper ringlets from it. You've never seen anything like it. Laugh! We couldn't stop. We told everyone but when we came back at night to the dance there wasn't a shred of ribbon left. That horrible old man had taken every scrap of it down. And if you ask me, Jamie Innes, you helped him."

"But didn't you say anything to him?" Pilkie demanded.

"How can you say anything to someone who isn't there?" Andrea asked helplessly. "Mr. and Mrs. Innes were terribly upset, of course, but it was too late to do a thing about it."

Sara and Caroline came in carrying a coffee pot and a tray with cups, biscuits, milk and sugar on it.

"Oh, but my dears, you shouldn't have done that," Andrea exclaimed, dashing to take the tray from Caroline.

"Mum will be down in a minute," Caroline told them. "Put the tray on the window-sill and we can all sit up there and drink our coffee. What does Jamie say about the Scottish dance?"

"He's his usual miserable self," Andrea sighed.

"Well," muttered Jamie in self-defence, "it's not right, Englishmen in kilts." And he snorted with disgust.

"I don't see anything wrong with it," Edgar said.

When Aunt Sadie came in they told her and she was wildly enthusiastic.

"What a wonderful idea," she enthused. "You must have a piper. I wonder if Vincent would."

"Oh, Mrs. Innes, if only he would," Andrea exclaimed. "Why, if Mr. Innes comes dressed in his kilt and plays his bagpipes all the other men will just stroll around looking for stones to crawl under."

"I'll ask him," Aunt Sadie promised. "If not, I'm sure Jamie . . ."

"Play the pipes for the English!" burst out Jamie. "I would do no such thing!"

We all roared with laughter at the horrified expression on Jamie's face. I hadn't known that he could play the bagpipes and I wondered to myself if he could play Fergus's pipe and I made up my mind to ask him the next time we were alone together.

The rest of the week was filled with the endless racket of Andrea's friends. They came and went as they pleased, in giggling, shrieking groups. Wherever one went they were there talking in excited voices about the dance.

By Thursday morning Andrea's birthday cake, which was coming from a London baker, still hadn't arrived. Mr. Reid had phoned London about it and had been told that the bakery had sent it two days ago. But the postmistress at Gartleven furiously denied any knowledge of it.

"The minute I clap my eyes on the thing," she declared, "our Wullie will be off with it to Deersmalen, at the double. That right, Wullie?"

"Aye," said Wullie.

"There you are. Her Majesty's mails are alert in your service, sir."

The above conversation was related to us by a distraught Andrea early on Thursday morning. "Anything, but anything, less alert that Wullie would be impossible to find," she lamented. "What on earth are we going to do? How can I possibly have a twenty-first dance without a cake? Do you think if it comes today you could send someone over to Craig Garth to let us know? We're all going to Inverness for the day and we won't be back till night, but I know I

77

wouldn't sleep a wink if I didn't know the cake had come. You do think it will come, don't you, Mrs. Innes? I have utter faith in your judgment. If you say you think my cake won't come I'll just lie down and die, honestly I will."

"Of course your cake will come in time," Aunt Sadie assured Andrea, thus preventing her untimely death. "And if it comes today I'll send Jamie over to tell them at Craig Garth so that the good news will be waiting for you when you get back tonight."

"Oh, you are an absolute angel," Andrea enthused and flung her arms round Aunt Sadie's neck. "There'll be someone there he can leave a message with. Oh, there's Freddie!" Andrea squealed as a blast from a car's horn shattered our eardrums. "I must fly or his ulcer will be all up in the air again. He can't bear to be kept waiting." And Andrea dashed out of the house.

"What I like about you, Mum," Jamie said, "is the way you blithely promise that I'll go trotting round to Craig Garth as if it were a house at the end of the drive instead of nearly six miles away. You never seem to think that I have things of my own to do."

"I seem to remember that this week you are hardly what one might call a free agent," Aunt Sadie reminded him and Jamie said no more.

Late in the afternoon Sara and I were in Caroline's bedroom watching Caroline trying to alter one of her white school party dresses for Shona to wear at the dance.

"Keep still, Shona," Caroline said for about the hundredth time. "How can I possibly get the hem even if you will keep moving?"

"I'm not moving," Shona denied the accusation hotly. "I'm standing here like a statue. Ouch! Will you watch what you're doing with those pins, Caro. The dress will be covered with gore if you stick many more into me."

"If you would only stop wriggling," Caroline said patiently.

"Oh, I do loathe and abominate wearing your clothes, Caro. I just hate it."

"It would be over so much quicker if you would stand still."

"I *am* standing still," Shona said. "Do you know, I can just see what's going to happen to us. You'll marry a duke or an earl or something and you'll have masses of super clothes and after you've worn them twice you'll pass them on to me and all my life I'll never, ever have worn anything but your cast-offs."

"If you don't want me to alter this dress just mention it and I'll stop at once and Mum can do it for you."

"Oh no, Caro, not Mum," said Shona desperately. "You should have seen the dress Mum altered for me last year," Shona said to Sara and me, and she hid her face in her hands at the memory. "I'll stand like this, Caro, till you've finished. I'll hardly breathe but don't let Mum near it." And Shona drew in her breath and stood as stiff as a poker.

"Just keep like that then," Caroline said. "The hem's squint. I'll need to do it again."

The bedroom door opened and Jamie stuck his head round it.

"The cake's come," he said. "They're opening it up now. Do you want to come and see it?"

" 'Course," yelled Shona, grateful for any excuse to escape from Caroline and she dashed downstairs with the rest of us close on her heels.

Aunt Sadie was just lifting the cake on to the table. It was made in the shape of a huge pink rose. On the edge of its petals were twenty-one candle holders made like dew-drops.

"Worth waiting for?" Aunt Sadie asked.

"It's beautiful," Sara exclaimed.

"Too good to eat," I said.

"I bet it cost a pretty penny," Edgar said knowingly.

"Well, someone had better go over and tell them that it's come," Jamie remarked, "and since I know it is going to be me I shall volunteer."

"How right you are," Aunt Sadie said. "Go now and

if you hurry you'll be back in time to help me clear the cloakrooms out."

"You coming with me, Shona?" Jamie asked.

"Shona is coming back upstairs with me," Caroline said firmly. "If I don't get that dress done this afternoon it won't be ready for the dance."

"O.K., O.K., I'm not thinking of going with Jamie. Come, sister, back to the horrors of the torture chamber." Holding the pinned hem of her dress well out from her bare legs, Shona went back upstairs.

"I'll come with you," I said to Jamie.

"Right," he said. "We'll take the bridles up to the ponies. Save bringing them down when we're going that way anyway. All we've to tell them is that the cake has arrived?" Jamie asked his mother.

"That's all," she said.

"I honestly don't see why, when there are all those cars at Craig Garth, one of them couldn't have taken a run over tonight," Jamie grumbled.

"They've all gone to Inverness and you know that perfectly well," Aunt Sadie said. "Now off you go and do as you're told for once."

We collected bridles from the stable and a handful of oats each from the bin. Then we walked through the pines to the hillside. The ponies were grazing close by and they came towards us, ears pricked, eyes glistening greedily, expecting oats.

"You ride Maggie," Jamie said, catching the dun Hansel for himself. "She's better in traffic than Polly. Not that we're likely to meet much but we'll go down on to the road to Craig Garth and then if any cars pass us we can give them the message."

Maggie in her excitement to get at the oats pushed them out of my hand and hardly got any, but I managed to slip the reins over her head to hold her until I could get her bridle on.

We went over the hill and down to a rough rutted track.

"This," said Jamie, "is the road."

"Gosh!" I exclaimed. "No wonder we were so bumped about the night we came."

"Yes, it's pretty rough, but then nothing much ever uses it. Dad says he can remember when it was a grassy track and you could gallop along it. You'd bring your horse down if you tried it now."

"Is your father going to play the bagpipes for them tomorrow night?"

"He says he is. It's more than I'd do for them."

"I never knew you could play. Are you any good?"

"Not so bad. Dad taught me, but I don't practise enough."

"Can you play Fergus's pipe?"

"Yes. Fergus has no son and he's teaching me. He says that when he's dead the Horse will come for my piping. Until now I didn't want to believe him. I kept kidding myself that although the Horse wouldn't accept me now it would in the future, that I *would* be the next guardian of the Horse. But now that I know I won't be, the next best thing is to follow Fergus, to learn to pipe as he can and then some day the Horse may accept me as it does Fergus."

I felt desperately sorry for Jamie and thought how dreadful it must be for him to have hoped for all these years that he would be the next guardian and for a strange girl to arrive so suddenly and take away his hope. But I couldn't say I was sorry for I wasn't, I was glad, gladder than I had ever been about anything. "But Uncle Vincent couldn't manage without Fergus," I said.

"No," replied Jamie. "The guardian has always had a piper, a wise man, to help him."

The ponies plodded steadily on, their unshod hoofs falling softly on the dried mud of the road. A burn rippled along beside us, running a clear, peaty brown over smooth stones. As I rode, I thought about what Jamie had said and a great relief flooded over me now that I knew that I would never be left alone to tend the Water Horse, that I would always have Jamie or Fergus to help me.

"Just our luck," Jamie said as we reached the gateway to Craig Garth. "Not a bloomin' thing passed us. We should

81

have brought Polly. You only need to take her on to a road for hordes of cars to appear from nowhere. It's another mile to the house but at least we can trot," and Jamie urged Hansel into a trot.

Like a ship on a rough sea, Maggie lurched after them. Twice I nearly slipped off, until, abandoning my pride, I took my reins in one hand and a hunk of coarse black mane in the other.

In contrast to the overgrown wilderness of Deersmalen, the grounds of Craig Garth were beautifully laid out. There were smooth green lawns, flowerbeds glowing with colour and borders filled with carefully-pruned shrubs. One of the lawns was laid out as a miniature golf course and beyond it were two tennis courts wired in with high netting. The house itself was obviously much more modern than Deersmalen. It was rough-cast, Snow-cemmed to a glaring white. It had a green slated roof and the doors and window-frames of the large windows were a crude scarlet.

We trotted up to the front door. Jamie jumped down and handed his reins to me. He knocked on the front door and waited but no one came.

Twice he tried but there was no answer.

"I'd better try round the back," he said, and taking his pony he led the way round to the back door.

In the back yard an elderly woman was standing with a duster tied round her head. She had a carpet beater in her hand and was just about to renew her attack on two rugs hanging from a clothes line.

"Mrs. MacDougall," Jamie called.

She turned round. "Why, Jamie, I haven't set eyes on you for days. What with the folks all being here and it being Miss Andrea's birthday I haven't had a minute to call my own. But there, I dare say your mother will have been the same this last week. Tell her I'll be over to see her the minute I get the chance. And tell her Geordie McIntyre from the Faulds is getting married at Christmas."

"We're here to tell you that Andrea's birthday cake came this afternoon," Jamie interrupted her.

"Ah, that'll set the poor lassie's heart at rest. She's been worried stiff about that cake."

"Mum opened it and it's fine," Jamie told her.

"Will you be stopping for a wee cup of tea?"

"Not just now, thanks. I've to get back and rescue my things from the cloakroom cupboard before Mum gets her hands on them, but I'll bring Kay another day."

"This is one of your cousins?" Mrs. MacDougall said, smiling at me. "Pleased to meet you, my dear."

"Be all right if we go out the back way?" Jamie asked. "We can jump the wall on to the moor."

"Well, you've done it often enough before, though how you get past that muckle horse-box of Miss Andrea's beats me."

"The ponies breathe in when I tell them," Jamie said laughing.

"I'll believe that when I see it. Get on with you now and mind and tell your mother about Geordie McIntyre," Mrs. MacDougall called after us.

The path round the back of the house led through a rhododendron shrubbery. We had just turned the corner out of sight of the house when our way was blocked by a huge horse-box.

"Gosh," I said. "It is enormous."

"Isn't it," agreed Jamie. "When dear Andrea was in juvenile classes she had four or five ponies, show ponies, show jumpers and gymkhana ponies, then when she was too old for juvenile classes she thought all she had to do was change her ponies for horses and dash around the shows picking up cups the way she did with the ponies. The float she had used for her ponies was too small so her doting Papa rushed off and bought her this thing. It only took her a few months to discover that senior classes offered slightly more competition than the juvenile classes had done. So she sold the horses she had bought and looked around for a top-class show jumper. Found Flare Way and bought a one-horse trailer for him. She's never used the horse-box again and two summers ago it was driven up here with three new deer ponies in it and it's stayed here ever since."

"Does it still go?" I asked.

"Oh yes. Mr. MacDougall keeps it in running order but I shouldn't think anyone'll ever use it again."

"What a waste," I exclaimed in disgust.

"It's far too big," said Jamie scornfully. "When the Reids aren't here it's kept in the open hay shed, but when the house party is here they take over the hay shed for their cars and this poor thing is dumped out here. You'll need to put your head right down on Maggie's neck and kick like anything to get past. I'll go first and give you a lead. Hansel is used to it."

Jamie and Hansel squeezed through between the rhododendrons and the horse-box and I followed behind. Shutting my eyes I clung on to Maggie's mane and kicked with my heels as she pushed her unwilling way past the bushes.

Once the hazard of the horse-box was behind us the path led on through a little wood of rowans and silver birches.

"We need to jump the wall here," Jamie told me. "There's not much room for them to get up speed so be ready in case Maggie puts in one of her huge leaps. I'll go first."

The wall was about two and a half feet high and made of stones cemented together. Jamie rode Hansel at it and they cleared it with inches to spare. I turned Maggie and kicked her on at it. She did her bone-shaking trot right up to the wall then she screwed herself over it on what seemed to me to be an enormous leap. We came sailing down on the other side and I landed with my arms round Maggie's neck, my face buried in her mane but still triumphantly on top.

"I warned you," Jamie said, giggling heartlessly. "You've to watch her and make her take off when you want to or she always leaves it too late."

We cantered back over the hills to Deersmalen. As we neared the house we saw, riding away from us, the upright figure of Fergus. He was sitting astride Turk, his cloak hanging about him in long straight lines. Like shadows at

Turk's heels loped the two lithe, low shapes of the Grey Ones. Fergus had Turk's reins looped over his arm and as he rode he was playing his pipe. The soft music came to us in snatches, half imagined like the sound of a distant hunting horn.

"I didn't know Fergus was going tonight," Jamie said, making Hansel stand. "I thought he wasn't leaving until tomorrow morning. Now he won't be back for four days at least."

"Where's he going to?" I asked.

"To look at an island with the right kind of lochan on it. Just in case." Jamie's eyes were troubled as he gazed after Fergus.

A sudden wind blew from the hills, over us and down to live for a second in the dark branches of the pines. I shivered uncontrollably.

"Someone whistled for it," Jamie said, shuddering himself.

We walked the ponies slowly down the hill and I thought how, with Fergus's departure, Deersmalen and Uncle Vincent were left alone and unprotected and I wished desperately that he hadn't had to go; that we could turn our ponies and gallop after him and bring him back with us.

CHAPTER SIX

Early next morning the house was filled with the more artistically-minded of the guests from Andrea's house party. They arrived before we had reached the bacon stage of our breakfasts.

"Morning," Andrea greeted us, poking her auburn head through the kitchen window. "Shall we just go through? We've got everything with us, drawing pins and tartan and—oh, just everything. Two of the men are bringing in sackfuls of heather."

"That's right," Aunt Sadie told her. "Just go right in. I guess you should know your way by this time."

Andrea withdrew her head. "Thank you, Mrs. Innes," she called. We heard her rousing her followers and they all trooped down the passage past the kitchen door.

"Hurry up all of you," Aunt Sadie told us. "If today starts getting out of control it's going to be the most horrible muddle imaginable. Vin, you are going to play the pipes for them tonight, aren't you?"

"Yes, my dear," Uncle Vincent answered placidly. "I said I would and I will. There is no need to worry about it any more. Though once their jazz band gets warmed up I think my pipes will not be in any great demand."

"Oh, Vin, don't be so modest. You'll be the hit of the evening. I shouldn't be in the least surprised to see you surrounded by swooning teenagers."

Uncle Vincent raised his eyebrows in mock alarm. "In that case I shall need to preserve my energies for this evening. I shall retire to my study and under no circumstances am I to be disturbed. My honoured elder daughter shall bring me a little nourishment about one o'clock."

He beamed at Caroline and getting slowly to his feet marched out of the kitchen.

"But there's so much you could help us with. You can't just go and shut yourself away," Aunt Sadie called despairingly after him but it was too late, he had gone. "Men !" muttered his wife savagely. She ran her hand through her hair and surveyed what helpers were left to her. "It just means there's all the more for the rest of us to do. First we'll need to get this kitchen cleared up. The caterers from Inverness will be here any minute now."

Even as Aunt Sadie spoke there was a loud banging at the front door.

"Go and see if that's them, Caro. And the rest of you get this table cleared as quickly as you like."

"But all we've had is porridge," Edgar gasped.

"And that's all you'll be getting," Jamie told him. "We just don't eat today."

"It's men with cases of champagne," Caroline said, reappearing. "Where will they leave them?"

"Room next to the cloakroom," her mother told her. "I'll come and see to them if you'll get on with the dishes."

We had everything washed up and put away before the caterers arrived. They were two dark, greasy men and two waitresses. Immediately they reached the kitchen they swathed themselves in voluminous white aprons and set to work. From the three huge hampers they had brought with them they produced masses of delicious-looking food—cold roast chickens, succulent hams, boiled lobsters, prawns, shrimps and little glass jars of bright, strange-looking things that I'd never seen before. Then the two waitresses laid out rows of tiny, puff pastry cases and the two men began to fill them. With delicate care they placed a scrap of chicken here and a tiny button mushroom there, a pink shrimp curved round a green olive, a shred of ham covered a sprinkling of grated cheese.

Edgar was just in the act of conveying one of the mushroom-filled cases to his mouth when the larger of the two men whirled round on him. Brandishing a fork he yelled, "Get out, get out. It is not that I do not like boys, I hate them ! Boys with dirty fingers who eat what is not meant for them. Get out and stay out!" He shook his fork in front of Edgar's nose.

"All right, I'm going," Edgar said, backing rapidly towards the door.

I followed him out, carefully holding my hand over a chicken-filled savoury.

"Jolly good," Edgar said, licking his fingers, after we had eaten our spoils.

"Umm," I agreed. "Fancy being let loose on that lot tonight."

"Can't wait."

"What are you wearing?" I asked him, thinking that really I hadn't seen much of Edgar since we came to Deersmalen.

"Jamie's lending me a kilt. I'm going to feel a real mug dressed up in a skirt. Good job none of the chaps from school can see me."

"What's Jamie wearing then?"

"He's got three!" Edgar told me. "Imagine, three kilts!"

"Ah, Edgar!" Aunt Sadie exclaimed, bearing down upon us. "Just who I'm looking for. Jamie's waiting for you at the back door. You're both going to chop up some logs for me. Andrea seems to think that the fireplace would look better with logs piled in it. Not that you'll really see it once The Phabulous Pheather Jazz Group get themselves installed in front of it."

Unwillingly Edgar dawdled away to the back door, muttering rebelliously as he went.

"Go and see how they're getting on with the decorations, Kay," Aunt Sadie organised. "See if you can help them."

The hall was a litter of heather and tartan. At one end Andrea was standing on top of a ladder holding up a length of tartan cotton while a blond young man with adenoids was directing proceedings from the floor.

"Lower, just a leetle bit lower," he was saying. "We must get the line of the grained wood carried on in the sweep of the tartan."

Obediently Andrea lowered the tartan a fraction of an

inch and they both gazed critically at the result through slit eyes.

Pilkie was kneeling on the floor, twisting the tough heather stalks into rings. Caroline, Sara and two well-scrubbed youths were helping her.

"Do come and be most awfully decent and lend us a hand," Pilkie boomed down the hall to me. "We've just heard that the old man has pushed off for a few days so we're making up halos for all the dear departed hanging around us."

I walked down the hall towards them.

"You make a circle of wire," Pilkie said, demonstrating as she spoke. "And twist the heather round it. You use the fine wire to bind it on with, then leave a long stalk of wire down the back to make the halo stand up above their heads. Little ones for the foxes and great, thick, gorgeous ones for the stags. They'll need to wear theirs at an angle unless their horns unscrew. Ronnie, dear, do you think there's the remotest possibility that their horns might just come out?"

"At the double, scarper," cried one of the scrubbed young men, looking dubiously at the nearest stag. "Not really my line of country, you know."

Suddenly there was a deafening crash. Andrea's ladder had slipped on the polished wood, depositing Andrea and her tartan on to the floor. We all rushed down to where she lay moaning, surrounded by folds of tartan.

"Coffee," she groaned. "Bring me coffee."

"Don't just stand there," commanded the adenoidal blond. "Can't you hear the lady requires coffee."

"For us all, Freddie, dear," added Andrea weakly from the floor.

"At the double, scarper," cried out of the scrubbed youths, carried away by the thought of a break in the heather halo industry.

"Don't look at me!" I exclaimed as I realised that his rousing remarks were aimed in my direction. "I'm only a
89

cousin and anyway the kitchen is full of child-hating caterers."

Andrea extended a long arm from her shrouds of tartan. "Freddie, raise me up. Mrs. Innes is a very dear friend of mine and I never met a caterer yet who wasn't willing to oblige when coaxed."

Freddie pulled her to her feet.

"I depart," she said. "To return on my shield or with coffee."

Ten minutes later Andrea was back with a plate of savouries in one hand, a plate of chocolate biscuits in the other and behind her a waitress carrying a tray loaded with cups of coffee. Andrea set her plates of food on the floor and took the tray from the waitress and placed it carefully beside them. "That was frightfully sweet of you. Thank you most awfully," she said to the waitress and "Tea up!" she shouted to Freddie who was still brooding over the tartan at the other end of the hall.

"Going to be a bit of a bind, all that tartan," he said, coming down the hall towards us.

"Don't worry, Freddie," Andrea told him. "Just sit down here beside me and drink your coffee and we'll all come and help you afterwards."

"Did you have gorgeous presents?" Caroline asked.

"Absolutely wonderful. I still can't believe in half of them. I'm getting a sports car from the old man, my Dior dress for tonight from Mum, a forward seat jumping saddle from Mick . . ." The list was long and mouth watering and we all listened enviously. "I've been utterly overwhelmed," Andrea finished at last and turning to Pilkie she inquired how the halo-making was progressing.

We had a rushed lunch and the day hurtled on into evening. Andrea and her friends departed at about three o'clock, shouting goodbye and saying that they would see us all later. Aunt Sadie decided that the weeds round the front door should be removed for the occasion, so Shona and I spent the rest of the afternoon weeding.

When we'd finished we went into the kitchen to see if

we could scrounge anything to eat and one of the waitresses gave use two salmon sandwiches and a slice of fruit cake each. Jellies, trifles and bowls of fruit lay on the kitchen shelves in rich profusion. All the tables were loaded with plates of cakes and biscuits. Edgar, appearing behind us, grinned in anticipation.

By eight o'clock everything was ready. The food was all laid out on tables in the small room next to the dining-hall. Chairs were arranged in little groups down each side of the hall and the stands for the jazz band's music stood waiting in front of the fireplace. The stuffed stags stared regally down, ignoring as best they could the frivolity of their rakish halos. Midge, a flowered smock of immense proportions girded about her, was in charge of the ladies' cloak-room.

"And that is surely everything," Aunt Sadie said as she stood in the doorway to the hall. "Yes, I can't think of a thing we've forgotten."

"If you could think of it you wouldn't have forgotten it," Jamie said pertly.

"Brat!" exclaimed his mother, cuffing him lightly over the head. "Now off you all go and get changed. It'll be a pleasant shock to see you all looking clean for once."

"Mother!" Caroline exploded, her dignity wounded.

"And Jamie and Edgar, be sure to scrub your necks. You look to me as if you're changing into a new grey-skinned species of the human race."

I got into the bathroom first so that when Sara came back into our bedroom I had nearly finished dressing.

"Do you know," she told me. "I nearly didn't bring my dress with me. But Mummy made me bring it. She said that you never know when you might need a thing and she was right. Do you really like it?" Sara demanded, holding up the dress for my inspection. Ever since the dance had first been mentioned Sara had been urging me to admire her dress.

"It's a smashing dress," I said for what I hoped would be the last time and I looked enviously at it. "I just wish it were mine." All I had to put on was a rather tired-looking party dress.

"We're fabulously lucky the Reids having their dance tonight," Sara said, using an adjective acquired after a week of hanging around Andrea.

"Why?" I asked. "They'd have invited us anyway, even if they'd had the dance in September."

"Clot! We won't be here in September. In another four days we'll be back home."

I dropped the hairbrush I was holding with the shock of Sara's words. "Home," I echoed in amazement. I had almost forgotten that there was such a place. "But I can't go back," I said in dismay. Deersmalen was my home. The land around it was my land. I wanted to stay here for ever and ever with Uncle Vincent, Jamie, Shona and Fergus. To live as they lived, galloping the shaggy ponies over the moor, coming back at night to the welcoming fastness of the house permanent against time; to listen to the slow strong voice of Fergus; to watch Jamie's blue eyes fill with tears and his body twist in uncontrollable laughter; to run behind Shona as she sped, swift and light before me, her silver hair loose on her shoulders; and most of all I must be here with them when Uncle Vincent said, "It is time, I think, to go again to the Black Loch."

"But I can't leave here," I said. "I can't go back home."

"And what do you think you're going to do?" Sara asked me, laughing.

I had no answer for her. I knew it was impossible to make her understand. I thought of our trim white bungalow; of school; of Mummy's plans to send me to stay with a French family next summer; of Jackie Munro, my friend at the riding school. It all came flooding back in stunned remembrance. They were no part of me any longer. Deersmalen and the Water Horse were the real things, the only things.

"You don't think Aunt Sadie is going to keep you here for ever, do you?" inquired Sara mockingly.

"Oh, you don't understand," I told her. "You could never understand."

"All right, all right, don't go getting all worked up about it," Sara said in her primmest tones. "If you don't hurry I'm going to be ready before you."

Telling Sara that I couldn't care less, I pulled my yellow dress over my head. It looked worse on me than it had on the hanger. Just the opposite was true of Sara's frock. It suited her perfect'y. She twisted her hair up on top of her head and, peering into the little, dark mirror, she powdered her nose and put on pale pink lipstick. Watching, it occurred to me that perhaps Sara was really quite pretty, far prettier than I would ever be.

When we, at last, made our way down to the dining-hall the dance was in full swing. At the far end of the hall Uncle Vincent stood, the squarl and ring of his pipes filling the hall. He looked the very image of all I imagined a Highland chieftain to be. He was tall, black-bearded, broad shouldered, his skin bronzed and his grey eyes alight with the music. Most of the other men in the room looked as if they were wearing fancy dress but Uncle Vincent wore his kilt and black jacket with its winking silver buttons, his frothing jabot and his chequered hose with the proud assurance of his race.

"You can do 'Strip the Willow,' can't you?" It was Jamie's voice at my side.

"I think so. We've done it at school."

Immediately he grabbed me by the hand and I was part of the gay, swirling mass of dancers. Jamie burned with life. Light and quick he advanced and retreated, stamped and clapped and swung me round until the whole hall washed dizzily about me.

I danced on and on. I danced with Jamie and Freddie and with the well-washed halo makers and with young men I'd never seen before who came obediently in our direction, ordered by Andrea to give the Deersmalen children a dance.

Then the jazz band took over from Uncle Vincent and the mood of the evening changed. It grew louder and brasher. The jazz taunted with the promise of new freedoms and the casting away of worn-out conventions, and the dancers accepted the challenge as they spun and gyrated.

Jamie, Shona and I made our way to the buffet but the room was crowded with the older guests who were standing about talking and nibbling.

"I'll go and get three plates from the kitchen," Shona said. "Then we can pile them up with food and take them away and eat in peace."

She returned minutes later with three bread plates.

"Good big ones," Jamie said, taking one for himself and handing one to me.

We wandered round the tables, piling our plates.

"Got enough?" Jamie asked, and Shona and I nodded. "Right, let's go up to the balcony and eat it there."

We went along the passage and after a quick look round to make sure that there was nobody about to see us, Jamie opened a door which I had always thought was a cupboard. Shona and I squeezed in and Jamie followed, shutting the door from the inside.

"Watch your dresses don't rub against the steps as you're going up," Jamie warned us. "They're thick with dust."

We climbed up the almost vertical wooden steps which led us out on to the narrow balcony. Balancing our plates on the balcony rail, we leant over and looked down at the dancers below.

"What a collection," Shona muttered as she devoured a shrimp savoury. "Don't Sara and Caro look ancient. You'd think Sara was eighteen easily."

"Well, she is fifteen," I said. "I think she looks rather nice."

"So do I," agreed Jamie. "So does Caro, but you and I aren't so very much younger and we just look our usual selves."

"Cleaner," Shona said.

"Yes cleaner, but not different the way they do," Jamie mused, looking down at his elder sister jiving expertly with a mousy little man.

94

"It's something that just comes," I said.

As I spoke, the band finished playing and after a flurry of clapping the dancers waited to see what was going to happen next.

Mr. Reid, a short, balding man, wearing pebble-thick rimless glasses and the frustrated expression of a meditating toad, stood up and walked to the middle of the hall. Like most of the older men he had withstood Andrea's plea to go all Scottish and was penguin-staid in conventional evening dress.

He made a short speech saying how glad he was that everyone had come to celebrate his daughter's coming of age. He hoped that everyone was enjoying themselves and if they were not, the noise they were making was most deceptive.

While Mr. Reid was speaking the waitresses had been passing round glasses of champagne.

"Go down and bring ours up, Jamie," Shona pleaded. And Jamie ran down to the hall to return carrying a tray with three round, shallow glasses of champagne on it.

I took mine and held it by the thin stem, feeling sophisticated and Londonish. "What does it taste like?" I asked. "I've never had champagne before."

"Fizzy lemonade," Shona said. "We always have it at the Craig Garth dance."

Below, the hall doors opened and one of the waitresses pushed in a trolley with Andrea's rose cake on it. The praying hands of twenty-one candles throbbed about it. Andrea, glamorous in a dress of heavy cream satin, stepped forward and got ready to blow out the candles. "In one breath, now." "No cheating." "You show them your wind's not gone yet, old gel." The voices of her friends shouted encouragement. Andrea shook back her auburn hair and blew.

"One left," Shona said, but even as she spoke the twenty-first candle flickered and died.

The cries of congratulation broke into the strains of "Happy Birthday" and then into "For She's a Jolly Good Fellow."

"Now," said Mr. Reid, slipping his arm round his daughter's shoulders, "a toast to my daughter. 'To Andrea, all health and happiness in the years ahead.' "

"Health and happiness to Andrea," cried everyone. The champagne tickled at the back of my throat but the taste was disappointing. It was just like sweetish lemonade.

Everyone was crowding round Andrea, congratulating her and shaking her by the hand. She was smiling and laughing and clutching a huge silver key that someone had presented to her. The two waitresses were plucking out the candles and the dewdrop candle-holders and carving the rose into ordinary pieces of cake.

"Any minute now and you'll need to go down and bring up our cake," Shona told Jamie.

"What we need is a basket on a rope that we can let down," Jamie said.

"Like Saul at Damascus," I suggested, but Jamie ignored my Biblical knowledge.

"Edgar could fill it for us," Shona said.

"I don't see him anywhere." I searched for Edgar's pink, round face. "He must be there somewhere."

"Bound to be," Shona replied. "Jamie, go for our cake or we're not going to get any."

Obligingly Jamie went.

"I got three outside pieces," he said when he came back. "But before we eat it we'll have another toast. Shona and I always do." Jamie squared his shoulders and, lifting up his glass, said, "To the One of the Black Loch."

"To the One of the Black Loch," Shona and I echoed and we drank the toast.

"The old papers say that it was to the hall built on the same foundation as this one that the first piper came and took the Innes of that time to see the Water Horse," Shona said.

As I listened to her words, the desolation of my imminent departure came back to me in a chilling flood of remembrance.

"Do you realise that we go home in three days," I said bleakly.

"You'll be back," Jamie said. "You're bound to be. You belong here. Some day Deersmalen will be yours."

"But I don't want to go! I can't go back to school and pretend that it matters, hockey and Latin and the school play, ugh! It'll kill me." I propped my head on my hands and stared dismally down at the glittering kaleidoscope beneath me. I knew only too well how longing for Deersmalen would sweep over me when I sat suffocating at a school desk, and how, when the drone of the maths mistress's voice grated on my nerves, the vision of the Water Horse, rising miraculous and majestic from the dark loch, would fill my inward eye, making me ache with longing to be standing again on the shores of the Black Loch.

Everyone in the hall was standing about in groups, talking and eating their pieces of birthday cake. Not really tasting it, I nibbled at mine. The Phabulous Pheather Jazz Group had forsaken their posts. Uncle Vincent and Aunt Sadie were talking to the Reids.

As I watched, Andrea stepped into the middle of the floor and clapping her hands to attract attention said, "Listen everyone, listen." The buzz of conversation died down. "Buffy is now going to entertain us with a display of his amazing skill with the lasso. Ladies and gentlemen, a big hand for Buffy. Come on, Buffy. Now don't be shy. You're amongst friends." There was a burst of clapping as Buffy came staggering out into the middle of the floor tripping over his lasso as he came.

He was a little man with broad shoulders, slim waist and narrow hips. His legs were thin as sticks and bandy as the traditional cowboy's. He had a small rat face, a thin streak of moustache, large, curiously flat eyes and straight dark hair that was swept back in a greasy curve from his forehead to the nape of his neck.

"What's he going to do?" Jamie asked, coming to stand between Shona and I.

"Lasso things I suppose," I said.

97

D

At first Buffy acted the fool and then with a neat flick of his wrist the rope sprung through the air to fall over Andrea's shoulders pinning her arms to her sides. She was pulled, giggling and protesting, to Buffy's side before he would release her. Swiftly and accurately his lasso fell where it wished. The guests squealed in nervous anticipation, for once Buffy selected his victim and sent his rope snaking through the air there seemed to be no escape for the chosen one, run or dodge as they might.

"I can't see Edgar anywhere," I said. "He's just not there."

"Must be somewhere," Shona replied absent-mindedly. "Isn't Buffy good? You'd think the lasso was doing it all by itself."

"I don't like him," Jamie said. "He's cold and slippery, like a dead fish. Not the kind of person I'd want to have anything to do with."

"I don't remember him being at any of the other dances," Shona said.

"No," agreed Jamie. "And I wish he wasn't here this time either."

Buffy whispered something in Andrea's ear and she turned and pointed up at us. In the next second Buffy's lasso was whistling upwards.

"He's going to lasso us," Jamie breathed in a tone of outraged dignity. The circle of the rope was above us. Not over my head or Shona's but Jamie's. In the split second before the lasso settled over his shoulders Jamie put his arms up so that when Buffy tightened the rope Jamie's arms were free.

"What have I this time?" demanded Buffy. "A tender young grouse if ever I saw one, but how are we going to get him down?" Buffy turned to Andrea. "Shall we see if we can make him fly?"

Buffy tightened the rope still further until Jamie was pulled against the wooden rail that encircled the balcony. "Now jump," Buffy commanded.

Everyone was looking up now, wondering what was going

to happen next. Buffy took no notice of anyone except Jamie. His large, flat eyes were fixed unblinkingly on Jamie's face and his mouth was set in a sly leer.

"Come, Master Innes, don't tell me you're afraid. Let us see your wings."

In some strange way it was no longer a party turn being used to amuse the guests at Andrea's dance but a battle of wills between Jamie and Buffy. What had started as a joke had turned into something else.

"If he won't fly we must make him." Buffy gave another quick tug on the rope.

Jamie, his face set with fury, spoke for the first time. "Let me go," he shouted down. "Let me go or I'll set myself free."

"The young lordling is going to free himself now," Buffy said laughing and everyone laughed with him.

The laughter was too much for Jamie. He grabbed the skean-dhu from the leg of his stocking, the blade of the knife flashed and the lasso was cut through. It fell limp and lifeless at Buffy's feet. Jamie lifted the loop over his head and tossed it down contemptuously. There was a moment's awkward silence until Andrea, still standing at Buffy's side, shouted, "A cheer for Jamie Innes, the only man ever to escape Buffy's dread lasso." And everyone, glad to be told what to do, cheered. The Pheather Group, no doubt used to covering over difficult moments, reassembled and in minutes the hall was filled with jiving couples.

"You shouldn't have cut his lasso," Shona said in mild reproof. "It was only a joke."

"No it wasn't. He was trying to pull me over."

"If you'd laughed to begin with it might have been all right," I suggested. "You'd have hurt yourself falling from this height."

"I know," Jamie said darkly. "And what's more he knew it too."

"Oh, Jamie, really!" Shona exclaimed in exasperation. "Why would Buffy want to hurt you? He's never seen you in his life before."

100

"That's as maybe but he wanted me out of the way all the same." Jamie shrugged his shoulders. "Come on," he said. "Let's go and get someone to teach us to jive."

It was half past three in the morning before the last guests left. Aunt Sadie flopped down in one of the chairs and said that before she went to bed she would like a cup of tea. Caroline and Sara went away to make it. Sitting in the deserted hall, we all drank a cup.

"Where's Edgar?" I asked. "I never saw him all night."

"He was with Caro and me to begin with," Sara said. "Poor boy, he was bored stiff. I do think it's mean the way you three leave him alone all the time."

I saw Aunt Sadie glance sharply at Jamie and open her mouth as if on the point of speaking, but she must have decided that it was too late to start telling Jamie off, for she closed it again without saying anything.

"I did enjoy myself," Sara went on. "We had a marvellous time, didn't we, Caroline?"

"Yes," said Caroline. "I've never enjoyed a Craig Garth dance so much. The jazz group was superb."

"I thought your father's piping was the outstanding event of the evening," Aunt Sadie said, smiling across at her husband. "You were magnificent."

"Thank you, my dear."

"And Buffy was tremendous with his lasso," Caroline enthused. "Why on earth did you cut it, Jamie?"

"As I have already told the others, who didn't believe me, and I don't expect you to believe me either, Buffy was trying to pull me off the balcony."

"Oh, Jamie!" Caroline exclaimed in exactly the same tone of voice as his mother had used when Jamie told her. "What utter nonsense. It was only a joke. Fancy thinking he really meant it."

"I didn't like him from the moment I saw him and I just hope I never see him again," said Jamie firmly.

"I'm inclined to agree with you," murmured Uncle Vincent.

"I thought he was fascinating," Caroline said. "Andrea

101

met him in London. Of course he's much older than us, but quite, quite fascinating. He's been everywhere—Africa, Egypt, Iceland. He collects wild animals for zoos. They pay amazing prices for quite ordinary animals. Buffy was telling us all about it."

A cold fear clutched at my heart. The thought of a collector of zoo animals so close to Deersmalen filled me with horror.

"Anyway," Sara added, "he was very decent to Edgar. He spent ages talking to him. Jolly kind-hearted of him, I think. I mean it's not as if Edgar could have had anything to say that would have interested Buffy."

CHAPTER SEVEN

The giant voice of the brass bell sounded through the house, waking me from my nightmares about Buffy and the Water Horse.

Sara sat bolt upright. "What on earth's happening?" she demanded.

Grey light was leaking in through the weave of the curtains. I looked at my watch but it had stopped.

"Must be someone at the door," I said. "Who'd be here at this time? It's hardly light."

Again the bell clanged.

"They're in a hurry, whoever they are," Sara said.

As we listened, we heard Uncle Vincent's heavy footsteps batter their way downstairs.

"Bet he's mad being woken up at this time," I said, and I jumped out of bed, and, running across the room, I opened the bedroom door. Very faintly I could hear the low murmur of voices. "He's talking to someone," I told Sara, "but I can't make out what they're saying."

I ran along the passage to a window that looked down on the front drive. Parked in front of the house was Freddie's Jaguar. I couldn't imagine what Freddie could want. He had been one of the last to leave the dance which meant he had only been away from Deersmalen for an hour or two.

"Kay! What are you doing?" Aunt Sadie, wrapped in a pink wool dressing-gown, was standing behind me. "Go back to bed at once."

"The bell woke me," I said.

"It's no one for you or Vin would have told you. Now go back to bed before you get a chill wandering around with bare feet."

"It's Freddie," I told her. "What can he want Uncle Vincent for?"

"Freddie?" Aunt Sadie said in surprise, peering out of the window. "Well, it's his car all right but it's very strange Freddie coming back. The last thing he said to me was that he would sleep the clock round after the dance. Said he wasn't used to a fast life."

"What can he be doing back so soon?" I asked.

"No idea," said Aunt Sadie. "Now do go back to sleep, Kay, while I go and find out what's happening down there."

Reluctantly I returned to bed. Sara had curled up again and was almost asleep.

"It's Freddie," I told her but she only grunted. I lay listening but all I heard was Uncle Vincent coming back upstairs. Gradually my eyes closed and I slept.

When I woke again it was broad daylight and there was no sign of Sara. I washed and dressed in a shirt and jeans. Then I scrambled downstairs.

Only Aunt Sadie was in the kitchen.

"Good morning," I said. "Where's everybody?"

"Good morning, Kay. We've all had breakfast but we just let you sleep on. It seemed a shame to wake you when you didn't really need to get up for anything. Sit down and I'll fry you an egg and bacon."

I sat down at the table and began to fiddle impatiently with my knife and fork. I hadn't had a chance to talk to Jamie and Shona last night it seemed to me to be desperately important that we made a plan to keep watch on Edgar. I didn't think that Edgar would have gone to all the trouble of phoning a zoo or a museum to tell them about the Water Horse but I did think that with Buffy more or less on the doorstep the temptation might be too great for him.

"Perhaps I'll just have bread and marmalade," I suggested to Aunt Sadie.

"Not at all. I've got your bacon on and your egg won't take a minute," she said, as with infinite care she broke the egg into a saucer before slowly sliding it into the frying pan.

"What did Freddie want?" I asked.

"Bad news, I'm afraid," Aunt Sadie told me, flicking the hot fat over my egg as she spoke. "Mr. MacManus, our family solicitor, is seriously ill. Freddie brought a telegram telling us and asking Vin to go to Edinburgh as soon as possible as there were matters connected with Deersmalen that Mr. MacManus wanted to see him about urgently."

"It must be really serious asking Uncle Vincent to go all the way to Edinburgh just like that."

"He hasn't been well for a long time. He knew himself that his heart might get worse suddenly but we understood that all the Deersmalen affairs were quite straightforward just now. Something new must have cropped up, but there, that's always happening."

Aunt Sadie put my breakfast down in front of me.

"How will Uncle Vincent get to Edinburgh?" I asked, knowing that there was only one train from Gartleven per day and that it left early in the morning. "He'd be too late for the train."

"Freddie took him to Gartleven. He called back half an

hour ago to tell me that Vin just caught the train by the skin of his teeth."

"Then Uncle Vincent's gone?" I asked incredulously. I had been thinking that if Jamie agreed we would go to Uncle Vincent and ask him what he thought about Buffy and Edgar. "Oh, Aunt Sadie, why did he have to go just now?"

"He didn't want to, especially with Fergus being away," Aunt Sadie said. "But the telegram sounded so urgent and Mr. MacManus has been a friend of the family for so many years now that he couldn't very well do anything else."

"How did Freddie get the telegram?" I asked. I was suddenly suspicious. The whole thing was too neat, too convenient.

"The postmistress from Gartleven phoned it through to Craig Garth. She thought there would be someone there with a car and that that would be the quickest way to reach us, quicker than Wullie and his van."

I gobbled down the rest of my breakfast and hurried out to look for Jamie. Aunt Sadie thought he was outside somewhere but she wasn't sure where so I went round to the cobbled yard, calling his name as I searched. But there was no sign of him. The hens scraped idly about the yard and the tethered goat glared at me balefully.

I climbed up into the hay loft and looked out over the wilderness of Deersmalen's grounds. There was no human being to be seen.

Treading carefully on the rafters I crossed to the other window and peered out through the cobwebs in the opposite direction. Again there was nobody to be seen. I was just about to turn away when I saw Edgar. From this window one twist of the drive was visible. Edgar marched along it and on down the drive out of sight. I only caught a glimpse of him but I knew as surely as if he had told me himself that he was going to tell Buffy about the Water Horse. His shoulders had been set, his head carried erect. He was going somewhere with a purpose, and I knew from the way he

106

strode forward that he had made up his mind and nothing would alter it.

For a second I stood in a blind panic. There was no Fergus, no Uncle Vincent and I couldn't find Jamie. I must do something, now, myself. I must reach Craig Garth and Buffy before Edgar did. I must stop him speaking to Buffy alone.

I hurtled down the loft ladder, grabbed Maggie's bridle from its hook and ran out into the yard. I ran on breathlessly through the pines and out on to the hillside where the ponies were grazing. I called Maggie but she took no notice of me and I had to climb all the way up to her before I could catch her. It took me ages to get her bridle on but at last I scrambled up on to her back and we were ready.

"Now," I told her, "as fast as you like to Craig Garth," and digging my heels into her sides I urged her into a canter. Once I got her wakened up she was willing enough and we galloped nearly all the way to Craig Garth. I was sure I would be too late and that Edgar would be there before me. But I kept reminding myself that Edgar walking couldn't possibly be faster than Maggie. The only danger was if a passing car gave him a lift and then he would surely be there before me. The thought made me push Maggie on faster than ever.

I had followed the track over the hills which Jamie and I had taken on our way back from Craig Garth the day before yesterday. When I saw the boundary wall I slowed down and walked her up to it just to make sure there was no one about.

The little wood was deserted. I found the place where Jamie and I had jumped the wall and turning Maggie I rode a few yards away from it, then swung round and cantered her on at it. This time I was ready for her leap and we sailed smoothly over.

I trotted on through the wood and along the path between the heavy leaved, dusty rhododendrons. It wasn't until I was half-way through them and almost in full view of Craig Garth that I realised that the horse-box was no

longer blocking the path as it had been when Jamie and I
had delivered the message about Andrea's cake. Then suddenly the two things clicked in my mind. The horse-box
had gone. The horse-box that had been large enough to
hold five horses, the horse-box that would hold the Water
Horse.

Frantic with horror I kicked Maggie on to Craig Garth.
Swinging myself off her I took her reins over her head and
rapped as hard as I could on the stout wooden door. No one
came. I banged again on the door and kicked against it
with my feet. I thought I was making enough noise to rouse
the entire household but when I stopped the echoes drifted
into silence and still no one came.

Every minute Edgar was getting closer while I stood like
an idiot skinning my knuckles on the unyielding door.

I ran round to the front door dragging Maggie at rein's
length behind me. "Oh, get on, you beast, you," I muttered
between clenched teeth as I yanked at her reins trying to
make her hurry. I seized the heavy knocker of the front
door in both hands and crashed it up and down. The noise
exploded like a bomb.

I heard running footsteps and the door was opened. To
my relief it was only Mrs. MacDougall.

"What in heaven's name is the matter?" she began.

"I'm sorry," I gasped. "But it's terribly urgent."

"Hammering on the back door and then at the front!
Don't think I didn't hear you the first time but if you think
I'm here to run about after the likes of you, you're wrong.
Well, what do you want? I haven't all day to stand here
admiring the scenery. As I said to Mrs. R., just this morning, I said, it's all right for them that has the time to laze
about staring out of windows but it's not for me. I've my
duties to see to. And as I says to her I hopes I pleases because if not she can look elsewhere . . ."

Twice I'd tried to interrupt the torrent of Mrs. Mac-
Dougall's words but with no result.

"Mrs. MacDougall, stop!" I yelled and she stopped in
mid-sentence, her mouth round open at my rudeness.

"Oh, please, Mrs. MacDougall, I must find a man who's staying here. The one they call Buffy. It's terribly important."

"Don't you shout at me, my girl," Mrs. MacDougall began and I thought she was going to start again on one of her full flood tirades but she didn't. "Buffy," she said pondering the name, her indignation curbed by her curiosity. "And what would you be wanting with him?"

"Oh, I can't begin to tell you," I said. "But you must believe me. It is awfully important that I find him at once. It's a message from Jamie Innes," I lied.

"Why, you're the girl who was here with Jamie! Och, my eyes are dreadful these days. You're the cousin was with him when he came to tell me about Miss Andrea's cake. And you that like his father. Come on in and have a cup of tea."

"I haven't time. Please can you tell me where Buffy is? If you don't know I'll just need to try and find him for myself."

"Nasty, greedy, crawling little man as ever I clapped eyes on. I could tell you a few things about that one, so I could."

"Please, please, will you just tell me where he is?" I pleaded. It was like trying to use a telephone and getting nothing but a continuous buzz.

"Well, I don't know just exactly where he is, but he's gone and good riddance to him, too. Away in that muckle thing the size of a house side. They say he's away to catch some animal or other but pity help the poor beast he lays his hands on, is all I say."

"When did he go?"

"A bit ago now. I heard Miss Andrea saying goodbye to him."

"Did he tell her where he was going?"

"Mentioned something about stopping at Deersmalen to meet someone."

So that was where Edgar was going. I could have kicked myself for being so stupid. Why hadn't I followed Edgar instead of assuming that he was going to Craig Garth? By now he must be in the horse-box with Buffy, taking him to the Black Loch. I had to get back at once and tell Jamie. How had I been such an idiot? Why had I let Edgar out of my sight for even a second and most urgent of all what was I going to do now?

"If he's not here I must get back to Deersmalen at once," I said to Mrs. MacDougall. I pulled Maggie's head up from the grass where she had been grazing while we were talking. "Thank you. I'm sorry to have been so much trouble." And I sprang on to Maggie's back.

"Och, think nothing of it."

Digging my heels into Maggie's sides I forced her into life. "Get on with you," I shouted and waving goodbye to Mrs. MacDougall I set off for Deersmalen.

I cantered Maggie through the rhododendron shrubbery, between the slim trunks of rowan and silver birch we galloped. I grasped her mane with both hands, kicked hard and we flew over the wall and were galloping on across the hill slopes.

The pounding thud of Maggie's hooves beat in my ears, matching the mounting panic in my brain. The Water Horse was in dire peril. Already I had failed it once. I should never have let Edgar out of my sight. Even at the dance I should have stayed with him. Now I must get back to Jamie. He was the only one left who might know what to do.

Maggie flew the low stone walls like a steeplechaser. Taking off yards before the walls, she soared over them and landed far out on the other side. I knotted my fingers in her mane and clung on for grim death.

When we reached the pines around Deersmalen I pulled her to a standstill and slid to the ground. For a minute my legs would hardly hold me and I stood leaning against the sweating pony. Gradually the feeling came back to them and I was able to move. I took Maggie's bridle off, patted her neck gratefully and thanked her for bringing me safely back to Deersmalen. Swinging the bridle in one hand I dashed through the pines.

"Jamie," I yelled as I got nearer to the yard. "Jamie."

There was no answer. I hung the bridle on its hook and ran into the house.

Jamie was standing at the kitchen sink, filling the water jug.

"Wherever have you been?" he demanded. "I've been looking everywhere for you."

"Craig Garth," I gasped breathlessly. "I couldn't find you so I went by myself. Edgar and Buffy have gone to the Black Loch in Andrea's horse-box. They've gone to capture the Water Horse. We've got to stop them, Jamie. Now. At once. We've got to do something quickly but I don't know what."

"Edgar is in there eating his lunch," said Jamie. "And I've been watching him all morning."

I couldn't believe Jamie's words. "Are you sure?" I exclaimed. "Have you been with him all morning?"

"Well, nearly all morning. Mum sent him down to the end of the drive with the can of milk for Sandy Duncan but that only took him about half an hour. He's sulking because he says we ignored him last night."

"Jamie, do hurry up," Aunt Sadie's voice rang out from the dining-room.

"We'll need to go and have our lunch," Jamie said. "We'll think about Buffy afterwards. I don't see that he can do much harm because he can't possibly know where the Black Loch is, even if he has picked up rumours about the Horse."

"Jamie, what are you doing?" called Aunt Sadie and we both scuttled through to the dining-room.

Everyone was sitting round the table, eating, and there, next to Jamie's empty chair, was Edgar, placidly munching away.

"Kay, where have you been?" asked Aunt Sadie, taking the water jug from Jamie and filling her glass. "We waited for you until we could wait no longer."

"I'm sorry," I said. "I went for a ride and I got a bit muddled."

"You really shouldn't ride over the hills by yourself.

111

There are far too many dangerous bogs. Even men who've lived here all their lives have wandered into them and been trapped," Aunt Sadie said.

I said sorry again and sat down and began to eat my lunch.

Suddenly Edgar sneezed. I saw his face wrinkle up as he struggled to hold it back but it was no use. "Atishoo!" Instinctively his hand went to his trouser pocket. He grabbed a corner of his handkerchief and pulled it out. "Atishoo!" he sneezed again as he buried his face in his handkerchief.

When Edgar had pulled his handkerchief out of his pocket something else had fallen out. I heard the soft thud as it hit the floor. Jamie bent down and picked it up.

"Yours, I think," Jamie said as he handed it back to Edgar.

Edgar's face flamed crimson. "Give it back to me," he demanded. "You'd no right to touch it. How dare you go poking your nose into other people's business." And he snatched whatever it was away from Jamie and stuffed it back into his pocket.

"Edgar!" exclaimed Aunt Sadie. "Behave yourself at the table. What did you pick up, Jamie?"

Edgar gazed fearfully at Jamie as he waited for his reply. His face had gone deathly pale and his bottom lip was trembling.

"Oh, nothing much," Jamie said to his mother. "Just something Edgar dropped."

"That's right, it's nothing really," Edgar mumbled. Then he put his knife and fork together and pushed back his chair. "I'm not feeling very well," he said. "I think I'll go and lie down for a bit." He made to stand up.

"Oh, no you don't," Jamie muttered. "Sit down until we've all finished."

I thought for a minute that Edgar was going to cry. He sat pale and shivering, his eyes half closed.

"You don't look too well," Aunt Sadie remarked. She obviously hadn't heard what Jamie had said. "You just run along and lie down."

"I'll fill a hot water bottle for you," Sara said, looking anxiously at her brother. "You don't look very good."

Edgar shook his head. "I'll just stay here," he said.

"Do go and lie down if you feel like it," Aunt Sadie urged him but Edgar only shook his head and sat in silence until we had all finished our meal.

Then Jamie stood up and putting his hand on Edgar's shoulder said, "Perhaps you'll feel better if you come outside for a bit." And he dragged Edgar roughly to his feet.

"Here, watch what you're doing with my one and only brother," Sara said laughingly as she cleared the table. Edgar glanced up at her and I thought he was going to ask her for help. But the moment passed and Sara walked out of the door, carrying away a pile of dirty dishes.

"We'll go to the stables," Jamie said. He gripped Edgar by the back of his shirt collar and marched him out of the room. "Shona, Kay, come on," Jamie commanded.

Obediently Shona and I followed him out of the house, across the grass and into the yard. Jamie led the way to a crumbling shed stacked high with bales of straw. Once inside, Jamie released his hold on Edgar's shirt and Edgar slumped down on to the straw.

"Show the others what you've got in your pocket," Jamie ordered.

As if he had no will of his own Edgar put his hand in his pocket and brought out a thick wad of pound notes, doubled over and held together with an elastic band. Shona and I gazed dumbfoundedly at the money.

"Now tell us where you got it from," Jamie said.

Edgar sat pale and silent but I knew without being told where the money had come from. Edgar had sold the Water Horse.

"Tell us before I make you," Jamie threatened. "You needn't think we don't know. We can guess. What we want to know is exactly how much you told Buffy and what he's planning to do now."

Edgar swallowed and tried to speak but he only made a dry gasping sound.

Jamie walked across and stood over Edgar. "Tell me what you told Buffy," he said again. And as he stood over the cowering white-faced Edgar I realised fully for the first time how strong and unyielding was the love for the Water Horse that was bred in the chosen ones of the House of Innes. I remembered with awful clarity how the skean-dhu had flashed in Jamie's hand last night and how it had glittered as it slashed Buffy's rope. My television-primed imagination saw the knife flash again in Jamie's clenched fist, flash and glitter above Edgar's head.

"Edgar," I shouted wildly. "Tell him what he wants to

114

know. You'll need to tell him in the end. Don't be an idiot, Edgar. Tell him now." It wasn't the white-faced, sinning Edgar with whom I was pleading but Edgar Innes of the old days, Edgar my cousin, whom I had never particularly liked, but who had been part of nearly every summer holiday I could remember. The Edgar that was before Deersmalen and the Water Horse were. "Tell him," I beseeched.

Staring down at the money in his hands Edgar spoke. "It was last night I told Buffy. He was the only one of everyone at the dance that even bothered to speak to me," he said in a flat, low voice. "Even Sara got fed up and just left me. You all knew that I couldn't dance but not one of you cared. I'd been looking forward to the dance all day. All the excitement there'd been getting ready and then you all just ignored me until Buffy came up and started talking to me about trapping wild animals for zoos."

"And so you told him about the Water Horse," Shona interrupted scornfully.

"He mentioned it first. Andrea had told him that she'd seen a water horse when she was a child and somehow I just told him what I'd seen. It was the only thing that I could think of to tell him that he would be really interested in. I wanted him to stay with me so that I wouldn't be left alone again, sitting there all by myself with everyone staring at me."

"That's all you told him?" Jamie demanded. "Just how you'd seen the Water Horse? When did he give you the money?"

"I met him this morning at the foot of the drive. He gave me the money then." Edgar was sitting on a straw bale, his elbows on his knees, his face buried in his hands. "And I gave him my compass readings and a map with the way to the Black Loch marked on it."

"Compass readings!" Jamie caught his breath in sharply. "So you'd a compass with you, you beastly little rat." He lifted his hand to strike Edgar but let it fall again without touching him. "That means Buffy is on his way to the Black Loch now."

"He's taken Andrea's horse-box from Craig Garth," I said. "It had gone when I was there this morning."

Jamie turned to Edgar. "Get out and stay out for ever and ever, you dirty traitor."

Edgar stumbled across to the open doorway. He paused, one hand on the door jamb, then he turned and faced us.

"You can say what you like," he said in a strangled choking voice, "but I did the right thing. It's greedy and selfish of you trying to keep the Water Horse hidden away. As Buffy says it doesn't belong to you. It belongs to the world. Everywhere there are scientists and naturalists that should know about the Horse and be given a chance to examine it."

"You don't know what you're saying," Jamie spat out the words as if they were poison. "It's you and people like you who are afraid of anything like the Water Horse. What you don't understand you must destroy. Put it in a cage for fools to stare at. Kill it and dissect it and pin it out on a board with a label for each little bit. Anything that's different you would claw down until it's the same as yourselves, mean and petty and ordinary. And if you can't turn it into a mass like yourselves you would kill it rather than leave it alone to be free. You sold the Water Horse for money. You broke the solemn promise you gave my father and you broke faith with all the past generations of Inneses for a few dirty pound notes."

"I didn't, I didn't," Edgar screamed. "I didn't want the money. He made me take it. I only wanted other people to share the Water Horse. I didn't want the money. Take it!" He flung the money from him.

The elastic band burst and the pound notes fluttered down on to the stone floor. With a choking sob Edgar turned and ran away across the yard.

Jamie, Shona and I stood looking at each other while a breeze rustled the pound notes with the dry sound of dead leaves, about our feet.

CHAPTER EIGHT

We stood in silence. Edgar's words still echoed in my ears. I shifted guiltily from one foot to the other. "*You* made Edgar betray the Water Horse," the voice of my conscience accused. "If you had been nicer to him this might never have happened." And I knew from the look on Jamie's and Shona's faces that they were thinking much the same thing.

Jamie moved first. He stepped towards the door, shrugging his shoulders and pushing back his light hair from his eyes. "What are we standing here for like a lot of stuffed dummies? We've got to get to the Black Loch."

"But what can we do when we get there?" demanded Shona.

"Everything," stated Jamie. "Once we're there we'll find some way of saving the Water Horse. There's nothing we can do here and every minute Buffy is getting nearer and nearer to the Horse."

"Are there roads?" I asked. "He's in the horse-box. He'll need a pretty good road to drive on."

"A year ago he couldn't have got near the loch. There was what they called a road but it was only a track really but now there's a tarmac road runs past the marsh, only about three miles from the loch itself. It's meant to attract tourists."

"There's still the three miles of bog," I said.

"It's not bog, only marshy, and it hasn't rained since the day we set off with Fergus," Shona said.

"We're still just standing here," Jamie exclaimed. "For goodness' sake let's get a move on."

"But what are we going to do?" repeated Shona. "It's no good rushing off in a panic."

"First," said Jamie, ticking the points off on his fingers as he spoke. "We must get the map from Dad's study. The island that Fergus has gone to see is marked on it. If we can get to the Black Loch first we'll find some way of getting the Horse to the island. Dad bought it so that we'd have a place to take the Horse to if the road did bring tourists. Just exactly how we'll get the Horse to the island I don't know. It all depends on whether it allows Kay to handle it without Dad being there. But once we get there we'll find some way, I know we will."

"Right," I shouted. "Uncle Vincent's study." All sense of guilt over Edgar had vanished and I was left with only the surging necessity of saving the Water Horse from Buffy.

We raced into the house. In Uncle Vincent's study Jamie opened the drawer of his father's desk and found the map we wanted. He spread it out and Shona and I leaned forward to see it properly. As Jamie's finger pointed to Deersmalen and moved to the Black Loch I could see in my mind's eye the route we had followed.

"That's the way we went and that's the road," Jamie said as he ran his finger along the red snake of the road. I was shocked at how much shorter it seemed than the way we had gone. "It's shorter," Jamie said, reading my thoughts, "but we never use it because of attracting attention. You see there's not much between it and the loch. And when it's dry the way it is just now you can cross the marsh without much trouble."

"Where's the island?" I asked.

"There," said Jamie pointing. "That one, Dad's marked it with red ink. About twenty miles from the loch, I should say. We've got to take the Horse there. With any luck, Fergus will still be there and he'll know what to do next." Jamie folded the map and stuffed it into his pocket. "You girls had better put something else on. It'll be cold, riding through the night. I'll go and get some food."

Shona and I hurried up to our rooms. The only jacket I had was the one for my suit. I opened my wardrobe and pulled it off its hanger. I wriggled into it and stood for a second looking round the room that had once seemed so bare and forbidding. Now it seemed safe and sheltering compared with the long night riding that lay ahead of me. Turning swiftly I dashed downstairs to where Jamie and Shona were already waiting.

"I've written a note to Mum and left it on her bedroom mantelpiece. I couldn't have explained to her. Here's what food I could scrounge." Jamie handed Shona and me a paper bag each. I took my bag and crammed it into my inadequate pocket. "Right?" Jamie asked and Shona and I nodded silently.

We ran to the stables where Jamie handed me Polly's bridle. He took Hansel's for himself and gave one to Shona.

"Biddy's?" queried Shona.

"Kay had Maggie out this morning, Fergus has got Turk and Minx is still going a bit short from his kick, so she's all there is. You're light enough for her anyway."

"What about the Water Horse?" I asked.

"Don't think a bridle would be any use," Shona said.

"A halter would be best," Jamie agreed. "Remember the time it cut its leg so badly, Dad had a halter on it then." Jamie pulled down a heavy rope halter from its hook and knotted it round his body.

We took oats to catch the ponies and Jamie filled one of his pockets with them in case the Water Horse would eat them.

In no time we were all mounted and riding away from Deersmalen. Shona was riding the little grey pony with the beige dapples. As we cantered over the grassy hillside excitement was tense between us. I certainly had no idea how we were going to get the Water Horse to the island and I suspected that Jamie wasn't too sure either. I wished with all my heart that Uncle Vincent or Fergus had been with us. Remembering the dark intensity of Buffy I was suddenly afraid of what we might find at the Black Loch.

We rode on holding our ponies in to a slow canter, each of us conscious of the miles that lay ahead. We cantered for as long as we could but at last the rough ground made us slow down. The ponies, damp with sweat, were glad to walk.

"It's quicker if we cut down on to the road here," Jamie told us. "We can trot as long as we keep on the grass verges and it cuts out the huge circle we'd need to make if we kept to the hills."

Soon we saw the tarmac road ahead of us, looking strangely alien and sophisticated in this wilderness of rock and heather.

"Better keep Polly on the inside," Jamie said. "I'll go first and then you and Shona with Biddy next to the traffic."

But Biddy never reached the road. As we made our way down towards it she stumbled badly on the loose stones, took one step forward and nearly fell.

"What's up with Biddy?" Jamie asked looking back impatiently.

Shona urged Biddy on but again she nearly fell. She was dead lame. Shona slid to the ground, took Biddy's reins over her head and made her walk forward. Unwillingly Biddy staggered after Shona. She was absolutely and completely lame. Shona picked out her feet and felt her legs but she could see nothing wrong with her.

"You'll need to go on without me," Shona said, disappointment making her voice shaky.

"You can't go back all that way by yourself," I gasped. "Try keeping her moving, perhaps it'll wear off."

Shona tugged at Biddy's head again but this time the pony came down on her knees when she was forced to move.

"It's useless," Jamie said. "You'll just need to take her back slowly. Will you be O.K. by yourself?"

Shona looked back the way we had come and I knew she was imagining herself struggling home through the dark. "'Course," she said. "I'll stay here for a bit and see if Biddy gets any better. Don't you waste any more time."

"Right," said Jamie reluctantly. "I'd let Kay stay with you but she's our only hope for leading the Horse."

"Don't be daft. Of course Kay must go with you. I'll manage fine myself. Get on and stop fussing."

Jamie and I turned our ponies and left her. We reached the road and settled our ponies to a steady hound jog. Their

120

unshod feet making no noise on the grassy verge. I glanced back to where Shona sat on a rock, shading her eyes to follow us. There were only two of us now. We were like the ten little coloured boys. First Fergus had gone, then Uncle Vincent and now Shona. "And then there were two," I murmured to myself. I looked at the slim figure of Jamie riding at my side and I thought how slight and defenceless he looked. Yet he had beaten Buffy at his own game last night and I remembered the smouldering hatred in Buffy's dark, flat eyes when Jamie had cut his lasso.

Jamie rode deep in thought. He spoke only when his thoughts became too urgent to be contained in silence.

"This isn't a game, you know," he said as we jogged along. "If Buffy is as unscrupulous as I think he is, he could make thousands out of the Water Horse. And he'd know the right people to take it to, the people who'd offer him the most money."

"It's stealing," I said. "He's no right to touch the Water Horse."

"I know," Jamie agreed. "But once people find out about the Horse it won't make any difference whether it's stealing or not. It'll be too late then."

Few cars passed us and Polly didn't really bother about the ones that did. There was no sign of the horse-box but we passed a family of tinkers camping at the roadside and Jamie asked them if they had seen it. They told us that it had passed a while ago. So we knew that at least we were on the right track.

The miles were marked by little white humped stones. Each one seemed farther apart than the one before. My legs and back ached and throbbed but Jamie trotted on relentlessly. As we rode the light began to fade. The sun burned a liquid disc above the line of the hills, sinking slowly down and drawing the colour from the earth. I wondered how Shona was getting on and I imagined her, tiny amidst the vastness of the moors, wearily trudging back to Deersmalen, leading her lame pony.

On and on we trotted. Without a saddle there was no way

of easing my aching body. I could do nothing but bump up and down to the willing Polly's stride. When a car passed us now it had its lights on, making Polly jump and peer, and the dark crept in closer when the bright lights had swept past.

"About another hour of road," Jamie said, grinning into the darkening night. "And then we cross by the side of the marsh to the Black Loch."

"Is there a chance we'll be there first?"

"Not a ghost of one. But there's bound to be tracks to follow."

"How will he catch the Horse?" I asked.

"Who knows," said Jamie grimly. "The Horse grazes at the edge of the marshland. The least sound will send it back to the loch but if Buffy tracked it silently enough he could lasso it then."

"But it'll fight," I said, seeing in my mind's eye the latent power and strength of the Horse.

Jamie shrugged his shoulders. "They catch elephants, don't they?" he asked irritably. "I don't know how they do it but if they can capture elephants I'm quite sure Buffy will find some way of taking the Water Horse."

It was dark now, the only light coming from the half moon. At last we turned off the road on to a narrow sheep track. The ponies picked their way cautiously along it. Now we were walking I took my bag of food out of my pocket and opened it. Inside was a squashed mixture of broken biscuits, sausages, savouries and crumbled cake left over from last night's dance. I ate two sausages and a handful of the savoury, cake and biscuit assortment. Then I twisted the ends of the bag together again and pushed it back into my pocket.

"Only about five miles more," Jamie called back to me. "How do you feel?"

"I don't," I said. "I've gone numb."

The ponies toiled on. I put my hands under Polly's mane to warm them, for the night was cold and I longed for my

Harris tweed hacking jacket instead of the skimpy one I was wearing.

At last we reached the loch. Its waters lay still as jet under the night. There was no sign of Buffy.

"Do you think we're here first?" I whispered to Jamie. It seemed too dangerous to speak aloud with the threat of Buffy's presence lurking in every shadow.
on, let's go down to the shore."

Jamie shook his head. "The most I hoped for was that we might catch him at it. I think the Horse has gone. Come

"If he's got the Horse out of the loch there's bound to be signs of a struggle," I said.

We walked the ponies slowly along the loch side. My nerves were stretched tight with anticipation. A duck spurtled up from the reeds just in front of us and I had to stuff my knuckles into my mouth to stop myself screaming out loud. I still could hardly believe that a horrid little man like Buffy could possibly capture the Water Horse. I searched the still loch waters for any sign of the Horse, hoping beyond hope, that I would see its proud head rising up from the loch. But Jamie's eyes were fixed on the shore. It was as if he knew that the Horse had gone and our only hope now was to track it down.

Jamie was right. We had almost reached the opposite end of the rocky shore when he jumped off Hansel.

"There you are," he said bitterly. "He's got the Horse all right. Look at that."

I slid stiffly down from Polly and staggered over to Jamie's side. The shingle at the loch's edge was crescented with hoof-prints. At first regular and peaceful, then changing from panic-deep prints to shingle torn and raked by the fighting force of the Horse. Then there was a wide crushed track of a heavy, inert body being dragged away.

"Doped," said Jamie, and in the same flat, cold voice he added the word I hadn't even allowed myself to think of, "or dead." Jamie crouched down, examining the tracks. "He's brought something on wheels down to here, loaded the Horse on to it and taken it back over the marsh."

I led Polly over towards the marshland and I could dimly make out the marks of wheels sunk deeply into the soft ground.

"We'll let the ponies go," Jamie said, "and follow the tracks on foot. Hansel would only kick up a fuss if he scented the Water Horse and anyway there's less chance of Buffy seeing us on foot."

Jamie was taking off Hansel's bridle as he spoke. I undid Polly's throat lash and noseband but hesitated before I actually took her bridle off.

"Will that be O.K.?" I asked. "Just letting them go like this, I mean."

"Oh, yes. They'll find their way back to Deersmalen. Probably be home by the morning," Jamie called back over his shoulder as he hurried away.

Quickly I slipped Polly's bridle off and with a hasty pat I left her and ran after Jamie. I had no wish to be left alone in this Buffy-haunted dark. For a second I couldn't see Jamie and my mouth went dry with fear. Then I saw him just to my right, bending down looking at the tracks again.

"It's been rollers not wheels," he said as I caught up with him. "And I rather think there's been another man with Buffy. Come on, everything depends on us catching up with them before they get away. Once they load the Horse on to the box and drive away we've had it. We'll have no idea where they've gone then."

"But if the Horse is dead?" I demanded. The night, the loneliness of the silent loch and the reaching waste of marshland made our task seem hopeless, impossible. What could we do against two men? If we had reached the loch first then we could have taken the Horse away to the island, but now . . . And if the Horse was dead what did it matter? Black depression filled my mind. "There's no use going on," I said aloud.

"Kay, what d'you think you're doing. For heaven's sake come on," Jamie's voice commanded me from the darkness.

Obediently I hurried after him. The broad trail of flattened reeds and grasses was easy to follow and Jamie ran

124

swiftly at the side of it while I struggled along behind him. While I had been on Polly I had longed to dismount and stretch my legs but now that she had gone I wished with all my heart that I was riding her again. I missed the security of her broad back, her surefootedness and her inborn knowledge of which marshy bits could be crossed and which were too boggy to be attempted. I ran blindly, reeds and tufted grasses catching at my feet. Twice I measured my full length on the ground and somewhere I must have dropped Polly's bridle because when Jamie offered to carry it for me I didn't have it with me any longer.

Running, jogging, breathlessly walking, we crossed the marsh back to the road. Always with the flattened trail leading us on. Sometimes the trail showed that whatever it was the men were dragging had become stuck in the soft ground and there had been a struggle to get it moving again. But always they had been successful and the trail continued into the night.

Car headlights swept over us and I realised that we were almost at the road. I opened my mouth to say something to Jamie but before I could speak he had grabbed my arm and pulled me down to my knees.

"What . . ." I began in surprise.

"Shut up," Jamie whispered furiously.

I strained my ears in the silence that followed but I could hear nothing threatening in the night sounds. Jamie put his finger to his lips, then turned and started back the way he had come. When we had gone a little way he stopped.

"Didn't you see it?" he whispered.

"No," I said. "See what?"

"When the car passed, its headlights lit it up."

"What?" I demanded again.

"Shh!" said Jamie staring back over his shoulder. Instinctively I looked around too but the black shadows cast by the moon remained motionless and no rope came snaking from the darkness to settle about my shoulders.

"See what?"

"The tent," said Jamie. "If we'd gone another three yards we'd have blundered right into it. I can't think how I didn't see it sooner."

"Do you think it's Buffy?"

"Might be anyone. I'm going back to find out," Jamie said and he began to creep silently back.

"I'm coming too," I muttered, determined not to be left behind.

"Then keep quiet," Jamie hissed.

I saw the white blur of the tent loom before us. We crept round to the back of it and waited listening. Inside someone was asleep, breathing heavily. The trail went on past the tent and after a few seconds Jamie beckoned me on and we slunk past the tent.

The trail stopped, was churned with men's footprints and then changed to the heavy, rutted tracks of the horse-box's wheels.

"They've loaded the Horse on to the box," Jamie said tensely. We followed the wheel marks to where the marshland ran alongside the road. To reach the road the horse-box would have had to climb a steep embankment of soft earth. We saw the deep scars in the earth where the box had tried again and again to reach the road.

"I don't think they've made it," Jamie muttered joyously. He was right. As we walked back along the roadside the wheel marks led away from the embankment and back towards the marshland and the tent. Cautiously we followed them until, rearing above us, huge in the pale moonlight, was the horse-box.

"It's still here," Jamie breathed and I knew from the relief in his voice that he too had been dogged by the hopelessness of our task. "At least we know now where the Horse is. If they'd got away from here we could never have stopped them."

"What now?" I asked.

"You wait here and I'll go closer and see what I can find out."

Jamie stole away from me and I hugged my arms about

myself, my ears sharp for any sound. I waited for what seemed hours then I saw a light flash in the cabin of the box. Terror flooded over me. For a second I waited, sure that the sound of Jamie fighting to free himself would shatter the silence of the night. I was tense, ready to run to his assistance, but nothing happened. Only darkness filled with intimate night noises and the thrusting enormity of my own harsh breathing filled my ears. Just as I was beginning to relax the crash of the cabin door being slammed shut made me jump and left my nerves tingling. A man's heavy footsteps were walking away from the horse-box in what I judged to be the direction of the tent.

Suddenly, silently out of the dark, Jamie was beside me. He grabbed me by the hand and started to hurry me towards the horse-box.

"Buck up. They must be taking it in turns to keep watch in the horse-box. That man's gone to waken Buffy, I think."

"But where are we going to?"

"To hide in the back of the box."

"But say there's nothing to hide under," I blurted out as I stumbled along.

"We've got to take the chance," Jamie muttered and hurried on.

Silently Jamie opened the door of the box and sprang up into the cabin. From below I could hear him feeling about for a door to let us in to the back of the box. My heart thumped painfully against my ribs. I was sure every second must bring Buffy striding towards us out of the dark. The skin at the nape of my neck was tense and ready for the cold clutch of his hand.

"Oh, do hurry, Jamie," I whispered, panicking.

Jamie didn't answer. Calmly his hands felt over the back of the cabin, searching for a door. Then I heard him catch his breath, followed by the click and squeak of a door opening.

"I've got it open," he breathed down to me. "Come on up quietly."

I hauled myself up into the cabin and closed the door as

quietly as I could. Jamie had already climbed over the seat and through the door into the back of the horse-box. I scrambled through behind him and fumbled with the door. It slipped from my fingers and banged shut.

"Idiot," Jamie muttered through clenched teeth. We waited, holding our breath, but no footsteps came running to investigate the noise.

We were on a high ledge above the actual box. I peered down into the darkness below me. "The Horse?" I demanded.

"It's down there," Jamie said. "It seems to be lying down."

"But is it alive?" I asked, afraid of Jamie's answer.

"Listen," said Jamie scornfully, and I heard what had probably been the first thing Jamie's sharp hearing had picked out when he climbed through the door, the short shallow sound of an animal breathing. I was filled with an immense thankfulness. We were not too late. There was still a chance.

"That's lucky," Jamie muttered. "Horse rugs. We can easily hide beneath these."

The rugs were piled in an untidy heap in the corner of the ledge, up against the back of the cabin.

"You get under first," Jamie said. "And I'll make sure you're hidden, then I'll join you."

I wriggled my way under the suffocating pile of horse rugs.

"O.K.?" Jamie's muffled voice reached me from the other side of the rugs. Then he too came crawling into the stuffy blackness. We sat with our backs to the cabin and our legs stretched out in front of us.

"Once Buffy comes back we won't be able to move an inch," Jamie said. "There's only this wood between us and him." Jamie rattled his nails on the thin wooden boarding between us and the cabin.

The sound of Jamie's nails on the wood had hardly died away before we heard light footsteps approaching the box.

"This is it," I whispered.

"Shhh!" said Jamie.

The cabin door was opened and someone whom we presumed to be Buffy sprang into the cabin, slamming the door behind himself. He opened the door into the back of the horse-box. We heard the clip of a torch being switched on and a little of its light seeped through the rugs to us. The torch was switched off, the door shut and we heard Buffy settle himself in the cabin behind us.

After half an hour my legs were an agony of pins and needles. I shifted my weight a little but felt rather than saw Jamie glaring his disapproval at me. After that I sat still and suffered it. It was rather like keeping your hand flat on a surface that is almost too hot to bear. The heat gets worse and worse but if you can just keep your hand there for a minute longer it starts getting less. The cramp in my legs was like that. Just when I though I couldn't bear it any longer my legs went numb.

My head nodded forward and I dozed. My mind wandered in dreams. Several times I half woke but nothing had changed and I slept on until I was wakened by men's voices.

I opened my eyes and saw that beyond the darkness of the rugs it was daylight.

"We're just going to move off," Jamie mouthed in my ear. "There are two of them and Buffy's driving."

CHAPTER NINE

Buffy started up the engine and the horse-box shuddered to life. He drove over the marshland to the road. Five times he drove at the earth embankment and five times the box sank into the clinging mud and would go no further until Buffy, swearing under his breath, backed the horse-box down and swung it round to try again. The sixth time the horse-box squelched up the embankment and with a sickening lurch struggled on to the metalled road. For seconds the front wheels clung to the road while the back wheels spun round and round in the mud. Then we crashed forward, free of the clinging mud, and the box was on the road.

I couldn't be certain, but I thought that we were travelling north, away from Deersmalen. The air under the horse rugs was almost non-existent and hunger gnawed at my stomach. I tried to get the paper bag out of my pocket, thinking it wouldn't be heard above the noise of the engine, but the crackling of the paper sounded even louder than the engine and I decided that it was better to be hungry than to be discovered.

Listening to Buffy and the other man, whose name was Joe, talking in the cabin, we learnt how they had captured the Water Horse. They had reached the loch side and lain hidden in the reeds until the grey half light brought the Horse out of the loch to graze at the water's edge. Buffy had lassoed it and Joe had shot it with a kind of dart which didn't harm the Horse but only made it unconscious.

Speeding along, Buffy whistled joyfully to himself. "Trust old Buffy," he crowed to Joe. "Meet a nice girl at a party, get myself asked to the Highlands for a sportin' holiday and I end up with an animal that any other collector would give his right arm to possess. Whenever I heard Andrea relating her party piece about the horse that disappeared into the loch I thought, Buffy, me boy, pin back your ear holes, there's more in this than meets the eye. 'Course I've come across these legends before in African tribes, the memory of an extinct species lingering on, but I knew this was different. The girl had seen it for herself. So I said to myself, Buffy, go and shoot grouse, there's no saying what a little spot of grouse shooting may lead to. Of course the boy was an absolute godsend. Without him we'd probably never have smelt the wretched animal. When I think how near I was to passing him by at the dance my heart fails me. Wait till Gilbertstein sees it. Hundreds of thousands he'll pay me for it or else he won't get it. Give Andrea a little something for the use of her transport. Might even send the old boy at Deersmalen a small cheque for services rendered. Wonder how he's getting on in Edinburgh?" Buffy roared with laughter. "Tried to put the young one out of action too but I didn't manage it. Still, can't be perfect." Buffy laughed again and went back to his whistling.

I felt Jamie stir triumphantly beside me. He had been right about Buffy's intentions.

Jerked and jolted in the back of the horse-box, I racked my brains to think what we should do next. As far as I could see, Jamie and I were powerless to do anything. In a way we were as much Buffy's prisoners as the Water Horse was.

"How do you feel about a bite of breakfast?" Buffy asked Joe abruptly.

"How does a ravening man-eating tiger feel about a man?" replied Joe.

"Right you are, then. Another half-mile and we pass the back road to the Lintore Hotel. We'll take this thing down to the back of the hotel where we can keep an eye on it and nip in for a decent breakfast."

A few minutes later I felt the box turn sharply right, and from the roughness of the road I presumed that we must be going along the back road leading to the hotel. The horse-box lurched and bounced, crashing down into pot-holes and knocking against stones.

"Some bloomin' road this," Buffy cursed as the box soared out of an especially deep rut.

Suddenly there was a screech of brakes and the box came to a violent stop. I was thrown forward and for a second I thought I was going to fall off the ledge and land down amongst the Water Horse. As I scrambled back Buffy's voice, loud with anger, reached us.

"What cussed fool left their bloomin' tractor slap in the middle of the bloomin' road. Some smash-up that'd have been if I hadn't stopped in time."

"Well, that's us had our breakfasts," Joe said dismally. "You couldn't get the box past that in a month of Sundays. Better back her up to the gateway we passed. You'll have room to turn her there."

There was a pause and I could hear Buffy drumming his finger-nails impatiently on the driving-wheel. "How about leaving her here while we dash in and get something to eat? My stomach is set on eggs and bacon."

Underneath the rugs, my mouth watered in sympathy with him.

"And we'll not touch another hotel for hours after this one."

"Who'd see it here, anyway?" encouraged Joe. "We'll lock the doors. No one could possibly see it. Half an hour and we'd be back."

"Would his lordship be prepared to wait for us?"

I heard Joe open the door to the back of the horse-box but this time he didn't just look through as Buffy had done, he came through, his movements sounding unbearably close. I was filled with unreasoning terror. I was sure that after our jolting about and the sudden stopping of the horse-box we couldn't be properly hidden. Perhaps Jamie's foot was sticking out from underneath the rugs or the top of my head was showing. Instinctively I put up my hand to pull the rugs more securely round me, but remembered just in time that a movement from underneath the pile of rugs would attract Joe's attention quicker than anything. I heard him jump lightly down and supposed that he must be examining

132

the Water Horse. It seemed an eternity before he leapt back up and squeezed through the door back to the cabin.

"How's things?" asked Buffy.

"Sleeping like a baby. I'll give it another shot when I come back. You know there's something weird about it. Hundreds of animals, one way and another, I've seen lying like that, out for the count and strapped down and I've

never thought a thing about them. Just animals and good riddance to them, I've thought. But that in there makes me feel guilty, to see it lying there. As if it was a person and somehow, somehow . . ." Joe struggled for words. "You'd think *it* was sorry for *you*."

"Ugh!" Buffy sneered. "You'll be suggesting next that we take it back and set it free. Not getting soft, by any chance?"

"What, me soft?" Joe denied the accusation hotly. "You

ought to know me better than that by this time. It's just that horse. Gives me the creeps, so it does."

"Come on and get some food before you start blubbing."

Joe and Buffy leapt down from the cabin, locking the doors. I counted up to sixty, swallowing between each number. Then I stuck my head out of the rugs and looked about me. Light leaked into the box through cracks where the wooden planks of its sides joined together. Jamie's face appearing from beneath the rugs loomed palely in the dim light. We shook ourselves free of the rugs and jumped down to stand by the Horse.

It was lying flat on its side, held to the wooden platform on which it had been dragged from the loch, by a broad leather surcingle and stout leather straps on its legs and neck. The jet blueness of its coat glimmered in the soft dark.

"How could they?" muttered Jamie bitterly, more to himself than to me. "How could they do it?" He crouched down at the Water Horse's head, running his hand through the warm denseness beneath the Horse's mane. "Do you know, this is the first time I've ever touched it?" Jamie said, looking up.

I nodded. I couldn't speak for the pity that tightened my throat. This was tragedy, the humiliation of the great, the mockery and scorning of a king.

"What now?" I asked, the words croaking in my throat.

"We've got to get the Horse away while they're in the hotel."

"Drag it, you mean?" I said, wondering if Jamie and I would ever manage to move the Horse, far less get it to safety before Buffy and Joe came back.

"No," Jamie said, pushing back his hair and standing up. "We could never drag it ourselves. Put the halter on while I undo the straps. Then I'll try to wake it."

Jamie handed me the halter, knotted out of thick prickly rope, which he had carried wrapped around him like a mountaineer's rope since we left Deersmalen. While we struggled with the stiff, heavy buckles, I eased the halter on to the Water Horse's head. I slipped its ears through the rope and ran the fine hair of its forelock through my hand to leave it lying straight and smooth down the Horse's forehead. Jamie struggled with the buckle at the Horse's neck and I knotted the halter rope so that it couldn't pull tight around the Horse's nose, choking and frightening it.

"Ready?" Jamie asked. "Then stand to the side and whatever happens don't let go of the rope."

"Shouldn't you open the horse-box first?" I asked, visions of the Horse crashing down the sides of the box and rousing Buffy, filling my imagination.

"No," Jamie said, "we'll give it a chance to settle in the dark."

I stood against the side of the box and waited. The rope was rough and heavy in my hands and I noticed gratefully that it was a long one, the type Jamie used when he was leading two or three ponies through a narrow gateway. I picked at its strands with nervous fingers as I watched and waited. So deep and far from life seemed the great bulk of the Horse that I could hardly believe that Jamie could have any way of bringing it back to the vibrant being I had touched on the banks of the loch.

Still crouching at the Horse's head, Jamie began to mouth the liquid music without words which Fergus had made in the cave on the night before the Water Horse had entered my life. With clear, seeking notes, Jamie's singing probed into the drugged mind of the Horse. Calling, waking, demanding, Jamie sang on but the Horse gave no sign of having heard. It lay motionless as a dead thing.

Suddenly the Horse moved. It shuddered and kicked back strongly with one of its hind legs. Jamie's voice rose loud and confident. The Horse opened dark eyes, lifted its head and Jamie's singing roused it and urged it on to greater efforts, demanded that it leave behind the doped oblivion which held its death, and wake to struggle for life. Arching its neck, its head flexed inwards, the Horse pulled itself up. For minutes it stayed like that, muscles tense, neck iron hard and crested, its forelegs stretched awkwardly in front of it. Poised between the struggle to stand and the release of collapsing back to negation. Then it surged up-right, exploding in the cramped space of the box.

"Speak to it," Jamie said, and I went up to the Horse's head and with my voice quiet and soothing I spoke gently. The Horse trembled as I came close to it and balanced its weight back on to its powerful quarters so that I thought it must rear upright, crashing into the roof of the box. I went on talking to it, hardly knowing what words I used, only knowing that in the absence of Uncle Vincent the Horse must accept me as guardian, must allow me to lead it to freedom.

I stood for long minutes dwarfed by the mass of the Horse, the sound of my pleading in my ears. Then suddenly the Horse sighed, relaxed and dropped its head to my hand.

I heard Jamie let out his indrawn breath in a sharp gasp. "I'll go and let down the ramp," he muttered. "We'll need to get a move on or they'll be back."

He jumped up and wriggled through the door into the cabin. In no time he was round to the back of the box and screwing down the ramp.

The daylight came to me first as a thread of white which grew to a blinding white stretch as Jamie craned the handle and the ramp was slowly lowered. The Horse stood with its head high, its ears pricked.

"Watch as you bring it out," Jamie called to me. "There's no one about but try to be as quiet as you can."

"Right," I called back and started to walk down the ramp. The Horse paused for a second then plunged forward, dragging me with it. I held on to the rope, gritting my teeth and expecting the Horse to try to gallop off when it reached the ground. But it didn't. It stood still, gazing around, its whole body tight with the strangeness and therefore the fear of its new surroundings. It looked as if the least sound would trigger it into instant flight.

Jamie craned up the ramp, making the Horse prance and peer suspiciously.

"Back towards the main road," Jamie said. "I know where we are. I was here last year with Sandy Duncan,

136

selling sheep to a farmer. The farm was the next road end past this back road to the hotel."

"Are you sure?" I demanded in amazement.

"Of course I'm sure," Jamie said, looking at me scornfully. "You don't think I'd forget a place I was at only last year? I knew where I was when I heard Buffy mention the Lintore Hotel. The men came to the hotel for a drink after they'd sold the sheep. Half-way along this back road there's a path that leads to the farm. We'll go that way now."

"But what about the farmer?"

"It's our only chance. Come on."

The Water Horse moved gigantic at my side. I held the halter rope but knew that really I had no control. The spirit of the Horse mastered mine. It was true and free, compact of such fire and power that no human could ever control it. Had it not been for the charm in the House of Innes the Horse would not have walked at my side but would save reared up, dragging the rope from my feeble grasp, and galloped free.

"Do you think you can get it to trot?" Jamie asked, looking back anxiously over his shoulder. "I spent hours trying to waken it and Buffy and Joe are sure to be back the minute they finish eating."

"I'll try," I agreed doubtfully.

"Go on, then," Jamie urged. "We've got to reach the track down to the farm before they get back to the horse-box or they'll see us."

I ran a few steps and the Horse broke into a trot.

"Good," breathed Jamie. "Oh, if you could only see it, Kay."

I couldn't see it but as I panted along I could feel the immense thrust and ease of the Horse's stride. Once I had ridden fit, clipped hunters from the riding school at home and felt in them their latent speed and strength, but compared to the Water Horse they had been as dead as the weariest of seaside donkeys.

We reached the path that led across the fields to the farm.

"Hurry," urged Jamie. "We've easily been half an hour

and I shouldn't think they'll stay in the hotel much longer than that. Can't you make it trot a bit faster?"

"I can hardly keep up with it as it is!" I gasped but I quickened the rhythm of my strides. I had got my second wind and was running easily in time with the Horse, my feet stinging as they slapped down on the dried mud of the path.

"There's the farm," Jamie shouted and pointed ahead.

"It's miles away," I said in dismay.

"Rubbish, it just looks a long way. It's not really."

I ran until I thought I could run no longer. My breath burnt in my throat and I staggered from side to side as I ran. At last we reached the farm, bursting like a hurricane into the dusty yard. At our approach, hens scattered squawking to the safety of midden and hayshed. A sow erupted from behind an open door, causing the Horse to stand up, striking out with its forelegs at the empty air.

"Don't let go," Jamie yelled.

"Don't worry, I shan't," I shouted back, twisting the thick rope round my hand and feeling like the prisoner in Byron's poem who was tied to the back of a mad runaway mare. "Wherever you go, I go too," I muttered, bracing myself against its struggles. At last it stood still again. But its head was thrown up suspiciously, eyes rolling, ears sharp, ready to light up again at the least thing.

"You'd better go and find the farmer," I said to Jamie. "See if he's got somewhere we can hide. Buffy's bound to come here looking for us and the sooner we get the Horse inside the better. It nearly got away from me then."

Jamie nodded and looking back at the tense Water Horse he hurried off to find the farmer.

Left alone with the Horse, I ran my hand down its powerful shoulder and spoke quietly to it, but it sprang back, irritated and watchful.

Jamie was back almost at once, bringing the farmer with him. He was a short, stout man, encased in the dirty shell of a thick tweed suit, the waistcoat of which strained at the buttons to cover his swelling belly. Below his knees his trousers were held in by leather straps. His feet were shod

138

with immense tackety boots, their upward curving soles giving him the gait of a rheumaticky rocking horse. A greasy cloth cap was pulled down over his face so that his eyes peered from its shade like sharp, darting insects with an independent life of their own. His face was tanned a dull shade of crimson and his cheeks and chin were covered with a flowering of white bristle.

They stopped a few yards in front of the Horse. The farmer settled his body on the thick stumps of his tweed legs. He stuck the rough stick he carried squarely in front of him and, resting both hands on the top of it, he leaned forward and squinted up at the Horse from under the brim of his cap. The Horse, glorious in its strength, gazed down at him.

"Aye, ye're right. It's some horse ye've got there," the farmer said, and spitting accurately to one side he went on staring up at the Horse while Jamie and I waited nervously.

"Ye'd best pit it in the front box. It's the yin I use fer the sheep but it's the biggest we've got and I think ye'll likely be needin' it." He led the way to a large door in an outhouse which faced on to the path we had just come down. He drew back a rusty bolt and putting his shoulder to the door pushed it open. "There, ye can pit it in there."

As I led the Horse forward I was wondering whether it would follow me into the darkness, but after one suspicious snort in the doorway it came willingly into the sheep-stinking box as if glad to be out of the light's glare.

"Can ye leave it?" asked the farmer.

"Oh, no!" I said. "I'll stay here. It's better with someone with it. Someone whom it knows. It's not used to being shut in anywhere."

"There's two men following us," said Jamie suddenly. "Two men who are trying to take the Horse from us. You mustn't tell them we're here." He stood with his shoulders squared, looking the farmer straight in the face, his words bursting out of him like bullets, so great was the urgency behind them. "The Horse belongs to us. They're trying to steal it from us. Please, please, don't tell them we're here."

139

No expression showed on the old farmer's face. He stood peering into the gloom of the box where the coat of the Water Horse shimmered like black ice to its every movement.

"Shut us in here and tell them you haven't seen us,", I pleaded. "Tell them you haven't seen anyone all morning."

"It's a guid thing for the two o' ye that the lad here kens Sandy Duncan or I might jist be wonderin' whit ye're daein' wi' a horse the likes o' yon beast. Aye, I might jist be wonderin' who exactly wis daein' the stealin'."

"You must believe us," Jamie said. "It's too late now for us to go anywhere else. They'll be here any minute."

"Aye, Bess can hear thim comin'. She aye kens whin onybody turns off the hotel road." He looked across the yard to where a rough-coated black and white sheepdog was sitting alert, her muzzle pointing along the path to the hotel. "But mind ye I've no onything agin' Sandy Duncan. He's a daecent fellow so long as ye keep an eye on him."

"Well, please for his sake shut the door and tell them you haven't seen us," I begged.

"Weel now, I'll no promise, ye ken, but I'll hide ye and see whit these two men have to say fer thimselves."

"Thank you," Jamie exclaimed. "Thank you very, very much."

Before I had time to say anything the farmer had stomped out of the box and pulled the door shut.

The only light in the box came from a small cobwebby window high in the roof. The smell of sheep rose sickeningly about us as we stood waiting, Jamie with his ear to the crack in the door and myself in the far corner with the Horse.

"They're coming," Jamie reported. "Running like mad. They're asking him now I think but I can't hear what he's saying."

"Try," I whispered back.

"I am trying," Jamie muttered and he crouched by the door, straining to hear. A grin spread over his face. "It's all right," he announced joyously. "They're fighting. I can

140

hear Buffy shouting at the farmer. He'll not tell them a thing now!" Jamie hopped from one foot to the other in a silent dance of victory.

Minutes later the farmer opened the door. "That's thim away," he announced. "Couple o' dirty, leein' tykes. I wisna long in seein' through they two. Offerin' me money as if I wis the dirt beneath their feet an' walkin' intae my yard

as if they owned the bloomin' place!"

"They've gone then?" I asked.

"Aye, thit they have and it's the polis'll be efter thim if I see hair nor hide of those two agin. I suppose ye'll no be efter refusin' a bite o' food? Ye don't look tae me as if ye'd be o'er weel supplied wi' the stuff."

He brought out morning rolls filled with crisp bacon and a mug of strong, black tea for us both. It wasn't until the mouth-watering smell of hot roll and bacon reached me that I realised just how hungry I was.

141

"It'll be a wee bit since ye've seen food," the farmer observed wryly as he watched Jamie and me devouring the rolls. "Ye're kinda wild o' the eye at the sight o' it." And chuckling to himself he stumped away, leaving us alone.

We watered the Horse and it drank thirstily, but when Jamie begged hay and oats from the farmer the Horse refused to look at them. It stood in the farthest corner of the box, its ears flickering to the least sound from outside, its eyes rolling wildly, showing white rims in the box's gloom.

We were prisoners until the dark released us. We couldn't risk taking the Horse about in daylight. We studied the map, trying to decide which would be the easiest way to reach the island. We had come more or less in the right direction and now only eleven or twelve miles lay between us and safety. A road and then a track led to the shore close by the island but I was sure that we would be safer going across country. Jamie, on the other hand, said there would be hardly any traffic on the road and we would be better to risk being seen than risk getting lost and wandering about in the dark.

"But cars passing us with their lights on would be certain to see us. They couldn't miss us. And say it was Buffy and the horse-box. We could never get away from them in time."

"We'd hide when we heard anything coming. At least we'd know where we were going if we stick to the roads. Wandering about in the dark on moors you don't know you'd probably end up back here in the morning or in a bog."

" 'Course we wouldn't, and just how do you intend to hide the Water Horse, that's all I'd like to know?" I asked contemptuously.

In the fetid dark of the loose-box we were almost quarrelling. Our nerves strained and on edge, we were each ready to take offence at the least thing. Everything Jamie said irritated me and I knew from the way he scowled and looked at me from under his eyelids that he was feeling the same way about me.

142

The day dragged on and we waited, sourly impatient, for night.

The farmer brought us more food at lunch-time and at tea-time. We thanked him, grateful for his kindness. Each time we ate what he'd brought and then went back to our listless, bored longing for the dark.

The Horse drank the water we gave it but still refused the oats or hay. All day it stood like a sentinel in the corner of the box, suspicious of every sound, utterly uncowed in the captivity of the box.

The day faded to dimness. The uneasy evening light changed to soft darkness. We thanked the farmer again for all his kindness, said goodbye and set off back to the main road.

The relief of escaping from the farm lifted our spirits and we hurried on through the dark, the Water Horse striding beside us. Reluctantly I had agreed with Jamie that perhaps he was right and we would be safer following the roads. So when we reached the main road we followed it until we branched off down a narrower road that would eventually lead us to the shore opposite the island.

"Once we get there," Jamie said. "You can stay with the Horse while I try to find a boat. I'm pretty sure Fergus will still be there and when I find a boat I'll row out and bring him back to the mainland then he can decide what to do next."

"Perhaps he'll see us from a great way off like the prodigal son's father and be there to meet us," I suggested hopefully.

Only two small cars had passed us on the main road. They had both sped by, their drivers bent over their wheels, looking neither to right nor left. And now surely we were safe. I walked relaxed beside the Horse, the rope held loosely in my hand. I still had some broken biscuits left in the bag in my pocket and as we walked I shared them with Jamie.

"If we keep up a good steady pace," Jamie said, "we should easily reach the sea by dawn. Just the best time to scrounge around for a boat. Nobody to see me. He crunched thoughtfully at a biscuit.

I wondered for the first time since we had left Deersmalen what Aunt Sadie would have to say about our disappearance and how Edgar would be feeling now that he had had time to think over what he had done. Then I remembered that Shona would be back at Deersmalen before us.

"What did you write in the note to your mother?" I asked Jamie.

"Said we were going camping again, only this time we didn't want Edgar with us so that when she read this we would be away and that it was important or we wouldn't have gone and she wasn't to worry about us."

"Poor Shona," I said.

"Perhaps Mum will wait until we're all there before she gives us a row. Anyway, Dad will understand. He'll explain to her."

"He'll be back from Edinburgh," I said, remembering suddenly about the false telegram. "It all seems so long ago."

"Doesn't it," agreed Jamie.

"But we've saved the Horse," I said, allowing for the first time a shiver of excitement and achievement to creep into my mind. I put my hand up and clapped the hard, muscled shoulder of the Horse. "Soon you'll be back with Fergus," I told it. "Soon you'll be free again."

Jamie heard it first. A sound no louder than the bumbling frustration of a bee on a window-pane.

"What's that?" I demanded.

"Shut up and listen," commanded Jamie, so that I knew he had already heard. The Horse threw up its head and stood stock still, immovable.

In seconds there was no hope that it might merely be the sound of traffic carried by the wind from the main road. The noise was the groan and strain of a heavy engine, the rattle and crash of metal, the spurt of loose stones from under speeding tyres.

144

"Hide," I screamed. "Quickly. We must hide some-where."

"Where?" said Jamie. "Where can we?"

"Anywhere, anywhere," I yelled, pulling with all my strength at the Water Horse's halter, but I might have been pulling at a leaden thing. The Horse stood rock solid.

My voice screamed again, "Jamie, do something, quick. We must get off the road before they see us."

But now the noise was close behind us. Headlights cut through the night, bursting about us like sudden pain, and like the intensity of pain they didn't pass but stayed blinding us, screeching about us. It was Buffy and the horse-box.

Brakes screeched. The cabin doors swung open and into the glare of the headlights jumped Buffy and Joe.

The Horse flung itself back against the rope and whinnied its panic into the night. There was nothing I could do but fight to hold the rope, to keep my feet, to stay in contact with the Horse. I saw the loops of the lasso held in Buffy's hand. I heard Joe shout, "Get it now, mate," and I knew this was the end.

Then, swift as a bullet, Jamie flung himself at Buffy's legs in a rugger tackle. At the impact Buffy staggered and fell while Joe seized Jamie by the legs and shook him like a rat.

The Horse surged against my weakening control, huge and jet black in the battering glare of the headlights.

Suddenly, as clearly as if he stood by my side, I heard Fergus's voice say, "Kay, you must ride the Horse."

I didn't think about it. If I had paused to think I would never have dared to do it, fear would have paralysed me. I slackened my hold on the rope. The Horse reared, soaring above me. When its forelegs touched the ground I was ready at its side. With the halter rope clenched in my left hand I sprang as I had never sprung in my life before. My body slapped against the sleek, hard muscle of the Horse's shoulder. My hands grabbed at its mane and sank deep into the matted, shaken hair. It leapt forward and as I wriggled upward, hauling myself on by its mane, pushing up with

145

elbows and knees and hip bones, I fought and struggled and gasped for breath.

After its first plunge the Horse beneath me was tight as a closed spring. With a final desperate effort I hooked my leg over its back, pulling myself up with arms that burnt like flame. I was on but only just in time. The Horse stretched out its neck, reached for its head and galloped free into the dark. I lay along its back, both hands twisted tight into its mane.

It seared the night with violence, and I, triumphant, rode the Water Horse.

CHAPTER TEN

I did not know for how long we had galloped or to where we were galloping. I could hardly remember who I was or what I was doing. As in a nightmare I was conscious only of the absorbing present, the strands of the Horse's mane cutting into my sweat-damp hands, the colossal play of the muscles in the Horse's shoulders and quarters as it strained and stretched in its panic-filled flight. We split through the silent night. The blackness seemed packed solid against our speed and the Horse flung back bow waves of ice-cold air as it breasted its resistance. I rode as the Valkyries ride, free of the earth. I had no idea if the Horse was still on the road or if it galloped over rocks and heather, or indeed if its hooves still touched the ground at all. I knew nothing but the ecstasy of our speed.

Gradually fear left the Horse. Its speed was a great but the desperate urgency of its first flight had died. As I crouched on its neck I began to wonder what I should do next; if I could reach the island by myself; where I would hide the Horse if I got there and what was happening to Jamie.

The Horse was cantering now at a loose, easy pace. I spoke to it and ran one hand up and down the crest of its neck. Quietly it changed to a slow trot and then to its long striding walk.

"If I get off now I might never get on again," I thought, remembering how I nearly hadn't managed it the first time. So I stayed where I was, balancing easily on the Horse's broad back. Steadily and purposefully the Horse walked on. I had no idea where we were going but the Horse seemed to know so I just sat there, glowing from the thrill of my gallop and being carried effortlessly on through the night.

The darkness grew thin. The first uneasy, questing light

147

probed at its obscurity, retreated, then returned more strongly. An opaque, chill greyness shrouded the earth. Yet still I could not see. The heavy, grey light was as blinding as the dark. Then, as if they rose from the sea-bed, rock and gorse, reeds and heather were created about me, and light seeped back. It was not yet dawn. Everything waited for the first freedom of the sun.

I rode stiff with the night's cold. I was lonely and tired and hungry. I longed for Jamie's company, but most of all I longed for Uncle Vincent or Fergus. No matter what I thought of, my mind returned to the one thought that if Fergus and Uncle Vincent hadn't left Deersmalen all this would never have happened. "Oh, if only they were here now," I thought. "They would know what to do." I leant down and rested my cheek against the sleek warmth of the Water Horse's neck. I had utterly no idea what I should do next. Vaguely I supposed that I should find somewhere to hide during the day. Even somewhere where I could leave the Water Horse while I tried to find out where I was. But I didn't want to do any of these things. Most of all I wanted Uncle Vincent and Fergus and next to them I wanted to creep into a soft bed and sleep.

I sat up, and putting both hands on the Horse's shoulders I stared about me at the rough moorland lying cold and colourless and mist-strewn. Uncle Vincent was too far away to be of any help but if only I could reach the island I would find Fergus.

"Fergus," I said aloud. "Fergus." As I spoke the first spear of the sun sprang over the mountains and crashed the world to life. And just as suddenly I knew where I was. True to its instincts the Horse was going back to the Black Loch.

For an instant I refused to believe my eyes, but there was no mistaking the waste marshland which lay ahead, nor the line of the mountains against the sky. The Horse knew it was close to its goal. Its ears were pricked, its neck arched and it walked out determinedly in the direction of the Black Loch.

148

I pulled wildly at the halter rope. "Stop!" I shouted. "You can't go back there. You've to go to the island, to Fergus. Don't you realise that if you go back there Buffy is sure to find you." The Horse tossed its head up and down as I tugged vainly at its halter. "Please, please stop," I pleaded, but the only effect I had on the Horse was to change its steady walk into a jog-trot. I seized the rope in both hands, pulling its head round to one side, then I kicked hard with both my heels. The Horse dropped its head, humped its back and bucked violently. I sailed skywards and landed with a thump on its back again. The Horse squealed with rage, leapt stiffly into the air, landed and sprang forward in a gallop.

I lay along its neck and in my last extremity I cried aloud to Fergus for help, almost believing that he might appear from nowhere to save the Horse.

The black waters of the loch streaked the edge of the marsh, the sheer fall of the mountains to the water's edge grew closer and still we galloped on. I was certain Buffy would be there waiting for us. He would think that I would fall off the Horse and that it would return to the Black Loch by itself. I imagined him as a great spider waiting for us to go blundering back into his web.

"Fergus!" I shouted, our speed tearing the words from my lips. "Fergus! Help me, Fergus."

The loch lay before us now, clear silver in the dawning light.

The Horse stopped stock still in mid-gallop and but for my handfuls of mane I would have gone flying over its head. With nostrils wide the Horse quested the air. Its ears flickered and twitched. It half reared and swung round to face the way we had come. Again it stood listening and seeking. I couldn't see or hear anything unusual. The thing that was so agitating the Horse was invisible to me.

With a screaming whinny it turned again and started back to the loch. Then, as suddenly as the first time, it stopped and again it stood tensely searching the empty air.

I felt it relax beneath me. It nickered softly and, turning

149

away from the loch, swung into a loping canter. Without hesitation or doubt it recrossed the marsh and turned right, over the moorland. I was so relieved that it had changed its course to worry much about why this had happened or what it would do next.

On and on the Horse galloped. Its long stride covered the ground with effortless ease. Although the land it galloped over was boggy and boulder-strewn it neither stumbled or paused in its pace. Every now and again it would nicker softly to itself, as if in pleasure and shake its head against the unbearable control of the halter.

My whole body ached with tiredness. I was afraid that sleep would overtake me as I rode and I would fall from the Horse, leaving it galloping on with the halter rope dangling dangerously amongst its feet.

The light grew clearer and stronger. Day was nearly here. The sun dazzled on a strip of flashing light seen for a second in a break between the hills. Straight as an arrow the Horse sped on, drawn relentlessly by some force I could not understand. Stone walls rose before me and fell away behind, yet I felt no change in the smooth stride of the Horse. No obstacle lessened our speed, no barricade could detain the winged purpose of the Water Horse. The land that had flowed past me, fluid as running water, became sharp and brittle with the sun.

We rose over the last of the encircling hills, and stretching away in a billion sparkling diamonds was an island-fretted sea. Without pausing, the Horse sped down towards it.

The sound was at first merely the wind as it snaked past my ears, then more insistent, more unmistakable. Stray wisps of sound that joined and linked and became the urgent fluting of Fergus's pipe.

The Horse raced along the flat sea verge. Wavelets curled milk smooth, crinkled and seeped in foam about its flying hooves. The sea, the early sunlight, the white curving wings of the gulls, the great shoulders and powerful neck of the Horse were all a glory and a joy. The Horse of the House of Innes was free and I, Kay of Innes, had saved it. I knew no words to contain my ecstasy but screamed my joy, as I galloped on, in a timeless, wordless pæan of praise.

The music of Fergus was now clear and strong and undeniable. And then I saw him standing out darkly against the sea dazzle. He was waiting by the shore, his pipe to his lips, his cloak loose about him. At his heels the Grey Ones lay, heads on outstretched legs, ears erect triangles. In the

water close by him a rowing boat danced lightly to the tide's movement. The Horse saw Fergus and whinnied with a deafening roar, thundering out its delight, and we plunged on towards him.

When the Horse reached Fergus it sighed from its very heart and laid its head on Fergus's shoulder, safe and at peace after all its miseries.

Tears misted my eyes and I could only sit twisting the halter rope in my hands, choking on the lump that swelled in my throat, and struggling to find something to say to Fergus.

"You have done well, Kay. You did not fail. When the day comes you will make a fit guardian for the Water Horse and under your care Deersmalen will come again to its old splendour." Fergus's eyes looking up into mine sparkled with green and peat-brown lights.

"If it hadn't been for you," I mumbled. "I didn't know what to do, Fergus. If you hadn't called the Horse I could have done nothing." I shivered, suddenly cold in the morning air, remembering my helplessness as the Horse galloped back to the Black Loch.

"Ah, do not be afraid, child, you will never be without help." A smile of infinite gentleness softened Fergus's gaunt features. "But come now, for I must be away to the island."

He held out his arms to catch me as I dropped from the Horse's back. My legs collapsed under me and I crumpled down on a boulder, too stiff and aching to move.

Fergus slipped the halter off the Water Horse's head and it sprang back, free at last. On the shore it reared and bucked and plunged. The sun glinted upon its jet black coat with lines of white light that flowed like tongues of fire to the play of its mighty muscles. Then, with a shrill scream, it trotted into the sea. For seconds it flirted at the water's edge. Lifting its legs high as a hackney's, kinking its tail, dropping its head to blow and squeal over the travelling froth of the wavelets.

It reared up, straight and high, striking out with its forelegs against the golden orb of the sun. Then swift as an unleashed dam it burst into the deeper water until it breasted the sea and it was swimming, every powerful stroke taking it farther from land.

I was filled with a great sense of emptiness and loss. I hardly saw Fergus, followed by the Grey Ones, climb into the boat and row after the Horse. It was all over. I would never ride the great Horse again. The reality must fade to a dream.

Now only Fergus's boat was visible, yet as I strained my eyes to follow it before it disappeared behind the nearest island I was sure I saw a black head rise by the side of it. Burning visionary in my mind's eye I knew the proud arch of the neck, the soft denseness of the fall of the mane, the lustre of the eye and the beauty of the line of the face from forehead to soft muzzle. As I stared even the boat was gone. The gulls screamed their eternal fishwife clamour, the sun threaded the glinting sea with extravagant beauty and I was utterly alone.

I sat staring out to sea while the morning ripened into day.

Over the road from the hills a scarlet Post Office van rattled down. I turned and watched it as it came along the shore road. It was broad daylight now but I had no idea of the time. My watch had stopped ages ago. Someone was leaning out of the van window, anxiously searching the shore for something. It was a boy, a boy whose fair hair blew in the sea breeze. It was Jamie.

I sprang to my feet and waved my arms wildly in the air. "Jamie," I screamed. "Jamie."

He saw me and waved. The van stopped to let him out and then hurried on its way again. Jamie came rushing towards me.

"Where's the Horse?" he was yelling. "Did it get away from you? Where is it?" He stood flushed before me. "Tell me what's happened."

"It's safe," I said. "It's with Fergus. He's taken it to the island."

"Oh, Glory! Glory! Glory!" Jamie shouted. "From the look on your face I was sure you'd let it go. We've saved the Water Horse!" And he sprang and flipped and doubled in ecstatic handstands and cartwheels. He seized me by both hands and whirled me round and round. "We've saved the Water Horse! We've saved the Water Horse!" he cried in joy. As I spun dizzily round my loneliness left me and I too was filled with the triumph of our achievement. "We beat Buffy," Jamie cried, letting me go so that we both sat down suddenly on the shingle. "Go on," he commanded. "Tell me."

153

I told him and he listened in silence, lying flat on his back, staring up at the sky.

"You rode the Water Horse," he said longingly. "Oh, Kay, why couldn't it have been me?" For a minute he was silent, struggling in his own mind with the question that no one could answer. Then he sprang to his feet. "What's it matter?" he said. "As long as the Horse is safe with Fergus. The man in the G.P.O. van said he'd look out for us on the way back and give us a lift to Lintore and from there we should manage to hitch a lift to Gartleven."

"What did Buffy do when he realised we'd got away?" I asked as we walked back to the roadside.

"They just abandoned me and tried to follow you. You must have left the road pretty quickly because they went after you at a terrific speed with Buffy hanging out of the window his lasso at the ready. In the end I think they went back to the Black Loch, hoping the Horse would head back that way. Least they passed me going in that direction. I wandered about over the moors shouting for you, then I decided that it was useless. When I got back to the road it was just getting light and I walked on towards here. It was while I was walking that the horse-box passed me, going towards the Black Loch, but they didn't see me. Then I got a lift from the van and here I am. Oh, Kay, I can hardly believe it. The Water Horse is safe."

"They'll never find it on the island," I said.

"Fergus will stay with it. While he's there nothing can harm it," Jamie assured me.

The G.P.O. van took us to Lintore and from there we got a lift in a telephone van that took us all the way to the road that ran past Deersmalen.

In the dim grey evening we jumped down from the van and thanked the driver, a huge, kind, walrus of a man who peered at us through thick lensed glasses. "That's O.K.," he said when we thanked him. "But next time you have a day in the country how about taking some food with you?" He had given us sandwiches and lemonade when he discovered we had nothing to eat. "We will," Jamie said. "We were in

154

an awful hurry when we left. Goodbye and thank you again, very, very much."

Together we walked up the long drive to Deersmalen. Overhead the pines swayed and whispered, sighed and surged like the sea.

"Home," said Jamie, "is the sound of the wind in the pines. I couldn't live away from them. If Buffy had won we would have had to leave Deersmalen. Dad would never have stayed here if the Horse had gone. Thank you, Kay, for saving it."

"It wasn't just me," I said.

"Without you we couldn't have saved it," Jamie said decisively. "Look," he said changing the subject, "the ponies are back." There, grazing on the long grass at the edge of the pines, were the ponies. Only the dun, Turk, who was with Fergus, was missing.

"They're home too," I said contentedly.

Light flowed golden from the open front door and Shona ran to meet us.

"The Horse is safe. On the island with Fergus," Jamie called to her.

"Oh-h!" Shona gasped, standing still with relief. "Oh, thank you, thank you, thank you. I'm so glad. Oh, Jamie, I'm so glad I could cry."

"What did Aunt Sadie say?" I asked.

"Mad at first," Shona said. "But Dad's back now and it's all right."

Uncle Vincent had followed Shona to the door and he stood, black against the lighter hall, waiting for us.

"The Horse?" he asked.

"With Fergus," Jamie said, and standing in the hall we told him all that had happened.

"I can never thank you enough for what you have done nor tell you how proud I am of you both." From the shadowy landing, where he had been listening, Edgar turned and crept away from the light. "You have both proved yourselves worthy of the honour entrusted to you, worthy to belong to the House of Innes. Tomorrow you must return to your family, Kay, but some day you will inherit Deersmalen. I know the Water Horse will be safe with you." He paused and I looked up into his grey eyes, so like my own, but I could find no words to tell him that my whole life and energy and will belonged to Deersmalen and the Water Horse.

"My dears, where have you been? You're filthy! I've never seen you so dirty! Running off and leaving me that scrappy little note! Really, Jamie, I've been worried stiff."

156

Aunt Sadie, appearing from the kitchen, was in full flood, but Uncle Vincent must have told her where we had been for she obviously knew. "If I could have laid my hands on you when I read it I'd have tanned the hides off the three of you. And Shona coming back all that way by herself! Kay, dear, you look worn out. Go and clean yourselves up a bit and I'll have a good hot meal ready for you when you come down."

As I finished packing, a clock struck midnight. In another five hours I would need to be up and getting ready to leave Deersmalen. It was all over. Tomorrow night I would be back with Mummy and Daddy, hearing about their holiday on the Continent. Sara lay sleeping and, looking at her, I was amazed at how different our holidays had been. I ran my hand along the smooth-grained edge of the dressing-table. Tomorrow it would still be here but I would be miles and miles away. "I don't want to go," I muttered to myself. "Why should I go?" But I was only a spoilt child kicking against the inevitable.

I went to the open window and stood behind the curtains, looking out. There was nothing but utter blackness and the restless, searching, unending sighing of the pines. Tonight under the same sky the Water Horse was free, in its own element.

As I stood there I heard the resonant wing-beat of a bird through the darkness, gently at first, then more certainly, gathering strength as it drew nearer. For a split second I glimpsed the mothy whiteness of a swan. Its great wings pulsed the night. It passed, and soft as a drift of feathers the sound of its wing-beats was absorbed by the great silence of the night.

I ran on for a minute longer staring out into the primeval blackness, remembering as I stood, the speed and glory of the Horse. For a second I felt it surge beneath me, saw the swell of its neck before me, knew again the power of its being and I was filled with the utter certainty that one day I would return to inherit Deersmalen.

157

Slówly I shut the window and turned away. The curtains swayed behind me. I undressed, put out the lamp, and creeping into the high bed I slept.

'JINNY AT FINMORY' BOOKS

by Patricia Leitch

Armada Originals

FOR LOVE OF A HORSE

Red-haired Jinny Manders has always dreamt of owning a horse. When she rescues Shantih, a chestnut Arab mare, from a cruel circus, her wish seems about to come true. But Shantih escapes on to the moors above their home where Jinny despairs of ever getting near her again.

A DEVIL TO RIDE

Shantih, safe for the first time in her life, in the Manders' stable, is inseparable from her new mistress. But she is impossible to ride, and Jinny can't control her . . .

THE SUMMER RIDERS

Jinny is furious when Marlene, the brash city girl, comes to stay and insists on riding Shantih. But when Marlene's brother, Bill, gets into trouble with the local police, Jinny and Shantih are the only ones who can stop him being prosecuted.

NIGHT OF THE RED HORSE

When archaeologists come to Finmory to excavate an ancient site, Jinny and Shantih mysteriously and terrifyingly fall under the power of ancient Celtic 'Pony Folk'.

Armada

has a whole shipload of exciting books for you

Here are just some of the best-selling titles that Armada has to offer:

- ☒ **Gallop to the Hills** Patricia Leitch 50p
- ☒ **A Devil to Ride** Patricia Leitch 50p
- ☒ **Ponies in Peril** Diana Pullein-Thompson 50p
- ☒ **Jackie on Pony Island** Judith Berrisford 60p
- ☒ **Six Ponies** Josephine Pullein-Thompson 60p
- ☒ **Plenty of Ponies** Josephine Pullein-Thompson 60p
- ☒ **Armada Horse & Pony Quiz Book No. 2** Charlotte Popescu 45p
- ☒ **Stolen Ponies** Christine Pullein-Thompson 50p
- ☒ **Black Beauty** Anna Sewell 50p
- ☒ **Zoo Quiz Book** Gill Standring 45p

Armadas are available in bookshops and newsagents, but can also be ordered by post.

HOW TO ORDER

ARMADA BOOKS, Cash Sales Dept., GPO Box 29, Douglas, Isle of Man, British Isles. Please send purchase price of book plus postage, as follows:—

    1—4 Books .... 8p per copy
    5 Books or more .... no further charge
    25 Books sent post free within U.K.

Overseas Customers

    1 Book: 10p. Additional books 5p per copy

NAME (Block letters)

_____

ADDRESS

_____

_____

_____